THE BRIDE
FONSECA NEEDS

THE BRIDE FONSECA NEEDS

BY

ABBY GREEN

First published in Great Britain 2015
by Mills & Boon, an imprint of Harlequin (UK) Limited,
Large Print edition 2015
Eton House, 18-24 Paradise Road,
Richmond, Surrey, TW9 1SR

© 2015 Abby Green

ISBN: 978-0-263-25681-9

CHAPTER ONE

'WELL, WELL, WELL. This *is* interesting. Little Darcy Lennox, in my office, looking for work.'

Darcy curbed the flash of irritation at the not entirely inaccurate reference to her being *little* and fought against the onslaught on her senses from being mere feet away from Maximiliano Fonseca Roselli, separated from him only by an impressive desk. But it was hard. Because he was quite simply as devastatingly gorgeous as he'd always been. More so now, because he was a man. Not the seventeen-year-old boy she remembered. Sex appeal flowed from him like an invisible but heady scent. It made Darcy absurdly aware that underneath all the layers of civility they were just animals.

He was half-Brazilian, half-Italian. Dark blond hair was still unruly and messy—long enough to proclaim that he didn't really give a damn about anything, much less conforming. Although clearly along the way he'd given enough of a damn to become one of Europe's youngest 'billionaire entrepreneurs to watch', according to a leading financial magazine.

Darcy could imagine how any number of women would be only too happy to watch his every sexy move. She did notice one new addition to his almost perfect features, though, and blurted out before she could stop herself, 'You have a scar.'

It snaked from his left temple to his jaw in a jagged line and had the effect of making him even more mysterious and brooding.

The man under her close scrutiny arched one dark blond brow and drawled, 'Your powers of observation are clearly in working order.'

Darcy flushed at being so caught out. Since when had she been gauche enough to refer to someone's physical appearance? He had stood to greet her when she'd walked into his palatial office, situated in the centre of Rome, and she was still standing too, beginning to feel hot in her trouser suit, hot under the tawny green gaze that had captivated her the first time she'd ever seen him.

He folded his arms across his chest and her eye was drawn helplessly to where impressive muscles bunched against the fine material of his open-necked white shirt, sleeves rolled up. And even though he wore smart dark trousers he looked anything but civilised. That gaze was too knowing, too cynical, for *politesse.*

'So, what's a fellow alumna from Boissy le Château doing looking for work as a PA?' Before she could answer he was adding, with the faintest of sneers to his tone, 'I would have thought you'd be married into European aristrocracy by now, and producing a gaggle of heirs like every other girl in that anachronistic medieval institution.'

Pinned under that golden gaze, she regretted the moment she'd ever thought it might be a good idea to apply for the job advertised on a very select applications board. And she hated to think that a part of her had been curious to see Max Fonseca Roselli Fonseca again.

She replied, 'I was only at Boissy for another year after you left...' She faltered then, thinking of a lurid memory of Max beating another boy outside in the snow, and the bright stain of blood against the pristine white. She pushed it down.

'My father was badly affected by the recession so I went back to England to finish my schooling.'

She didn't think it worth mentioning that that schooling had taken place in a comprehensive school, which she would have chosen any day over the oppressive atmosphere of Boissy.

Max made a sound of faux commiseration. 'So Darcy *didn't* get to be the belle of the ball in Paris with all the other debutantes?'

She gritted her jaw at his reference to the exclusive annual Bal des Débutantes; she was no belle of any ball. She knew Max hadn't had a good time at Boissy, but she hadn't been one of his antagonists. Anything but. She cringed inwardly now when she recalled another vivid memory, from not long after he'd first arrived. Darcy had come upon two guys holding Max back, with another about to punch him in the belly. Without even thinking, she'd rushed into the fray, screaming, *'Stop!'*

Heat climbed inside her at the thought that he might remember that too.

'No,' she responded tightly. 'I didn't go to the ball in Paris. I sat my A levels and then got a degree in languages and business from London University, as you'll see from my CV.'

Which was laid out on his desk.

This had been a huge mistake.

'Look, I saw your name come up on the applications board—that you're looking for a PA. I probably shouldn't have come.' Darcy reached down to where she'd put her briefcase by her feet and picked it up.

Max was frowning at her. 'Do you want a job or not?'

Darcy felt tetchy with herself for having been so impetuous, and irritated with Max for being so bloody gorgeous and distracting. *Still.* So she said, more snippily than she'd intended, 'Of course I want a job. I *need* a job.'

Max's frown deepened. 'Did your parents lose everything?'

She bristled at the implication that she was looking for work because her family wasn't funding her any more. 'No, thankfully my father was able to recover.' And then she said tartly, 'Believe it or not, I like to make my own living.'

Max made some kind of a dismissive sound, as if he didn't quite believe her, and Darcy bit her lip in order to stay quiet. She couldn't exactly blame him for his assumption, but unlike the other alumnae of their school she *didn't* expect everything in life to be handed to her.

Those mesmerising eyes were looking at her far too closely now and Darcy became excruciatingly conscious of her dark hair, pulled back into a ponytail, her diminutive stature and the unfashionably full figure she'd long ago given up any hope of minimising, choosing instead to work with what she had.

Max rapped out in Italian, 'You're fluent in Italian?'

Darcy blinked, but quickly replied in the same language. 'Yes. My mother is from just outside Rome. I've been bilingual since I learnt how to talk and I'm also fluent in Spanish, German and French. And I have passable Chinese.'

He flicked a look at her CV and then looked back, switching to English again. 'It says here that you've been in Brussels for the past five years—is that where you're based?'

Darcy's insides tightened at his direct question, as if warding off a blow. The truth was that she hadn't really had a base since her parents had split up when she was eight and they'd sold off the family home. They'd shuttled her between schools and wherever they'd been living which had changed constantly, due to her father's work and her mother's subsequent relationships.

She'd learnt that the only constant she could depend on was herself and her ability to forge a successful career, cocooning her from the pillar-to-post feeling she hated so much and the vagaries of volatile relationships.

She answered Max. 'I don't have a base at the moment, so I'm free to go where the work is.'

Once again that incisive gaze was on her. Darcy hated the insecurity that crept up on her at the thought that he might be assessing how she'd turned out, judging her against the svelte supermodel types he was always photographed with. Beside them, at five foot two, Darcy would look like a baby elephant! In weak moments over the years she'd seen Max on the covers of gossip magazines and had picked them up to read the salacious content. And it had always been salacious.

When she'd read about his three-in-a-bed romp

with two Russian models she'd flung the magazine into a trash can, disgusted with herself.

He suddenly stuck out his hand. 'I'll give you a two-week trial, starting tomorrow. Do you have accommodation sorted?'

Darcy blanched. *He was offering her the job?* Her head was still filled with lurid images of pouting blonde glamazons, crawling all over Max's louche form. Reacting reflexively, she put out her hand to meet his and suddenly was engulfed in heat as his long fingers curled around hers.

He took his hand away abruptly and glanced at a fearsome-looking watch, then back to her, a little impatiently.

Darcy woke up. 'Um…yes, I have somewhere to stay for a few days.' She repressed a small grimace when she thought of the very basic hostel in one of Rome's busier tourist districts.

Max nodded. 'Good. If I keep you on then we'll get you something more permanent.'

They looked at each other as Darcy's mind boggled at the thought of working with him.

Then he said pointedly, 'I have a meeting now, I'll see you tomorrow at nine a.m. We'll go through everything then.'

Darcy quickly picked up her briefcase and backed away. 'Okay, then, tomorrow.' She walked to the door and then turned around again. 'You're not just doing this because we know each other...?'

Max had his hands on his hips. He was beginning to look slightly impatient. 'No, Darcy. That's coincidental. You're the most qualified person I've seen for the job, your references are impeccable, and after dealing with a slew of PAs—gay and straight—who all seem to think that seducing the boss is an unwritten requirement of the job it'll be a relief to deal with someone who knows the boundaries.'

Darcy didn't like the fact that it stung her somewhere very deep and secret to think that Max would dismiss her ability to seduce him so summarily, but before she could acknowledge how inappropriate that was she muttered something incoherent and left before she could make a complete ass of herself.

Max watched the space where the door had just closed, rendered uncharacteristically still for a moment. Darcy Lennox. Her name on his list of potential PAs had been a jolt out of the blue, as had the way her face had sprung back into his mind with vivid recollection as soon as he'd seen her name. He doubted he could pick many of his ex-classmates out of a police line-up, and Darcy hadn't even been in his year.

But, as small and unassuming as she had been, and some four years behind him, she seemed to have made some kind of lingering impact. It wasn't an altogether comfortable realisation for a man who regularly excised people from his life with little regret, whether they were lovers or business associates he was done with.

Her eyes were still seared into his mind—huge and blue, a startling contrast to that pale olive complexion, obviously inherited from her Italian mother.

Max cursed himself. *Startling?* He ran a hand through his hair, leaving it even messier. He was running on fumes of exhaustion since returning from a trip to Brazil a couple of days ago, and quite frankly it would be a relief to have someone working for him who *wouldn't* feel the need to see him as a challenge akin to scaling a sexual Everest.

Darcy Lennox exuded common sense and practicality. Dependability. The fact that she had also been in Boissy, even if her time had been cut short, meant that she knew her place and would never overstep the mark. Not like his last assistant, who had been waiting for him one morning, sitting in his chair, dressed only in one of his shirts.

He tried for a moment to conjure up a similar image featuring Darcy. but all he could see was her serious face and her smart, structured shirt and skirt, the tidy glossy hair. A sense of relief infused him. Finally an assistant who would not distract him from the deal of a lifetime. A deal that would set him up as a serious player in the very competitive world of global finance.

Quite frankly, this was the best thing that had happened to him in weeks. Darcy would meld seamlessly into the background while performing her duties with skill and efficiency. Of that he had no doubt. Her CV was a glowing testament to her abilities.

He picked up the phone to speak to his temp and when she answered said curtly, 'Send all the other applicants away, Miss Lennox is starting tomorrow.'

He didn't even bother to reiterate the two-week trial caveat, so confident was he that he'd made the right decision.

Three months later

'Darcy, get in here—*now*!'

Darcy rolled her eyes at the bellowed order and got up from behind her desk, smoothing down her skirt as she did so. When she walked into Max's office and saw him pacing back and forth behind his desk she cursed the little jolt she always got in her solar plexus when she looked at him.

Virile, masculine energy crackled in the air around him. She put her uncomfortable reaction down to the fact that any being with a pulse would be incapable of *not* responding to his charisma.

He turned and locked that dark golden gaze onto her and snapped out, 'Well? Don't just stand there—come in.'

Darcy had learnt that the way to deal with Max

Fonseca Roselli was to treat him like an arrogant thoroughbred stallion. With the utmost respect and caution and a healthy dollop of firm-handedness.

'There is no need to shout,' she said calmly. 'I'm right outside your door.'

She came in and perched on the chair on the other side of his desk and looked at him, awaiting instruction. She had to admit that, while his manners could do with finessing, working for Max was the most exhilarating experience of her life. It was a challenge just to keep up with his quicksilver intellect, and she'd already learnt more from him than she had in all of her previous jobs combined.

Shortly after starting to work for him he'd installed her in a luxurious flat near the office at a ridiculously low rent. He'd waved her protests away, saying, 'I don't need to be worrying about you living in a bad area, and I will require you to be available to work out of hours sometimes, so it's for my convenience as much as yours.'

That had shut Darcy up. He was putting her there so she was more accessible to him—not out of any sense of concern because she was on her own in a city she didn't know as well as she might, considering her mother's Italian background. Still, she couldn't complain, and had enjoyed the chance to have a central base from which to explore Rome.

Max had been true to his word. She'd found herself working late plenty of evenings and on some Saturdays for half the day. His work ethic was intimidating, to say the least.

He rapped out now, 'What was Montgomery's response?'

Darcy didn't have to consult her notes. 'He wants you to meet him for dinner when he's here with his wife next week.'

Max's face hardened. 'Damn him. I'd bet money that the wily old man is enjoying every moment of drawing this out for as long as possible.'

Watching his hands, splayed on his slim hips, Darcy found it hard to focus for a second, but she forced her gaze back up and had to acknowledge that this *was* unusual. Most people Max dealt with knew better than to refuse him what he wanted.

His mouth was tight as he spoke almost to himself. 'Montgomery doesn't think I'm suitable to take control of his hedge fund. I'm an unknown, I don't come with a blue-blooded background, but worst of all, in his eyes, I'm not respectably married.'

No, you certainly are not, Darcy observed frigidly to herself, thinking of the recent weekend Max had spent in the Middle East, visiting his exotically beautiful lover, a high-profile supermodel. A little churlishly Darcy imagined them having lots of exotically beautiful babies together, with tawny eyes, dark hair and long legs.

'Darcy.'

She flushed, caught out. Surely working with someone every day should inure you to his presence? Not make it worse?

'It's just dinner, Max, not a test,' she pointed out calmly.

He paced back and forth, which threatened Darcy's focus *again*, but she kept her eyeline resolutely up.

'Of course it's a test,' he said now, irritably. 'Why do you think he wants me to meet his wife?'

'Maybe he just wants to get to know you better?

After all, he's potentially asking you to manage one of the oldest and most illustrious fortunes in Europe and his family's legacy.'

Max snorted. 'Montgomery will have already deemed me suitable or unsuitable—a man like that has nothing left to do in life except amuse himself and play people off each other like pawns.'

He raked a hand through unruly hair, a familiar gesture by now, and Darcy felt slightly breathless for a moment. And then, angry at her reaction to him, she said with not a little exasperation, 'So take...' She stopped for a moment, wondering how best to describe his mistress and settled for the most diplomatic option. 'Take Noor to dinner and persuade Montgomery that you're in a settled relationship.'

Max's expression turned horrified. 'Take Noor al-Fasari to dinner with Montgomery? Are you *mad*?'

Darcy frowned, and didn't like the way something inside her jumped a little at seeing Max's reaction to her suggestion. 'Why not? She's your lover, and she's beautiful, accomplished—'

Max waved a hand, cutting Darcy off. 'She's

spoilt, petulant, avaricious—and in any case she's no longer my lover.'

Darcy had to battle to keep her face expressionless as this little bombshell hit. Evidently the papers hadn't yet picked up on this nugget of information, and he certainly didn't confide his innermost secrets to her.

She looked at Max as guilelessly as she could. 'That's a pity. She sounds positively delightful.'

He made that dismissive snorting sound again and said, with a distinct edge to his voice, 'I choose my lovers for myriad reasons, Darcy, not one of which I've ever considered is because they're *delightful.*'

No, he chose them because they were the most beautiful women in the world, and because he could have whoever he wanted.

For a moment Darcy couldn't look away from Max's gaze, caught by something inexplicable, and she felt heat start to climb up her body. And then his phone rang. She broke the intense, unsettling eye contact and stretched across to answer it, then pressed the 'hold' button.

'It's the Sultan of Al-Omar.'

Max reached for the phone. 'I'll take it.'

Darcy stood up with not a little sense of relief and walked out, aware of Max's deep voice as he greeted his friend and one of his most important clients.

When she closed the door behind her she leaned back against it for a moment. What had that look been about? She'd caught Max staring at her a few times lately, with something unreadable in his expression, and each time it had made her silly pulse speed up.

She gritted her jaw as she sat down behind her desk and cursed herself for a fool if she thought for a second that Max ever looked at her with anything more than professional interest.

It wasn't as if she even *wanted* him to look at her with anything more than professional interest. She was not about to jeopardise the best job of her career by mooning about after him like she had at school, when she'd been in the throes of a very embarrassing pubescent crush.

Max finished his call with his friend and stood up to look out of his office window, feeling restless. The window framed an impressive view of Rome's ancient ruins—something that usually soothed him with its timelessness. But not right now.

Sultan Sadiq of Al-Omar was just one of Max's very small inner circle of friends who had given up the heady days of being a bachelor to settle down. He'd broken off their conversation just now when his wife had come into his office with their toddler son, whom Max had heard gabbling happily in the background. Sadiq had confided just before that they were expecting baby number two in a few months, and happiness had been evident in his friend's voice.

Max might have ribbed him before. But something about that almost tangible contentment and his absorption in his family had made him feel uncharacteristically hollow.

Memories of his brother's recent wedding in Rio de Janeiro came back to him. He and his brother weren't close. Not after a lifetime spent living apart—the legacy of warring parents who'd lived on different continents. But Max had gone to the wedding—more because of the shared business concerns he had with his brother than any great need to 'connect'.

If he had ever had anything in common with

his brother apart from blood it had been a very ingrained sense of cynicism. But that cynicism had all but disappeared from his brother's eyes as he'd looked adoringly at his new wife.

Max sighed volubly, forcibly wiping the memory from his mind. Damn this introspection. Since when did he feel *hollow* and give his brother and his new wife a moment's consideration?

He frowned and brooded over the view. He was a loner, and he'd been a loner since he'd taken responsibility for his actions as a young boy and realised that he had no one to turn to but himself.

And yet he had to concede, with some amount of irritation, that watching his peers fall by the wayside into domesticity was beginning to make him stand out by comparison. The prospect of going to dinner with Montgomery and his wife was becoming more and more unappealing, and Max was certain that the old man was determined to use it as an opportunity to demonstrate his unsuitability.

At that moment Max thought of Darcy's suggestion that he take his ex-lover to dinner. For some reason he found himself thinking not so much of Noor but of Darcy's huge blue eyes. And the way colour had flared in her cheeks when he'd told her what he thought of that suggestion.

He found himself comparing the two women and surmised with some level of grim humour that they couldn't be more different.

Noor al-Fasari was without a doubt one of the most beautiful women in the world. And yet when Max tried to visualise her face now he found that it was amorphous—hard to recall.

And Darcy...Max frowned. He'd been about to assert that she *wasn't* beautiful, but it surprised him to realise that, while she certainly didn't share Noor's show-stopping, almost outlandish looks, Darcy was more than just pretty or attractive.

And, in fairness, her job was not to promote what beauty she did possess. Suddenly Max found himself wondering what she would be like dressed more enticingly, and with subtle make-up to enhance those huge eyes and soft rosebud lips.

Much to his growing sense of horror, he found that her voluptuous figure came to mind as easily as if she was still walking out of his office, as she'd done only minutes before. He might have fooled himself that he'd been engrossed in the conversation with his friend, but in reality his eyes had been glued to the provocative way Darcy's pencil skirt clung to her full hips, and how the shiny leather belt drew the eye to a waist so small he fancied he might span it with one hand.

His skin prickled. It was almost as if an awareness of her had been growing stealthily in his subconscious for the past few months. And as if to compound this unsettling revelation he found the blood in his body growing heated and flowing south, to a part of his anatomy that was behaving in a manner that was way out of his usual sense of control.

Almost in shock, Max sat down, afraid that Darcy might walk in and catch him in this moment of confusion and not a little irritation at his wayward responses.

It was the memory of his ex-lover that had precipitated this random lapse in control. It had to be. But when he tried to conjure up Noor's face again, with a sense of desperation, all he could recall were the shrill shrieks she'd hurled his way—along with an expensive vase or two—after he'd told her their affair was over.

A brief knock came to his door and Darcy didn't wait before opening it to step inside. 'I'm heading home now, in case you want anything else?'

And just like that Max's blood sizzled in earnest. A floodgate had been opened and now all he could see was her glossy dark brown hair, neatly tied back. Along with her provocative curves. Full breasts thrust against her silk shirt. The tiny waist. Womanly hips, firm thighs and shapely calves. Small ankles. And this was all in a package a couple of inches over five feet. When Max had never before found petite women particularly attractive.

She wasn't even dressed to seduce. She was the epitome of classic style.

He couldn't fault her—not for one thing. Yet all he could think about doing right now was walking over to her and hauling her up against his hot and aching body. And, for a man who wasn't used to denying his urges when it came to women, he found himself floundering.

What the hell…? Was he going crazy?

Darcy frowned. 'Is there something wrong, Max?'

'Wrong?' he barked, feeling slightly desperate. 'Nothing is wrong.'

'Oh,' said Darcy. 'Well, then, why are you scowling at me?'

Max thought of the upcoming dinner date with Montgomery and his wife and imagined sitting between them like a reluctant gooseberry. He made a split-second decision. 'I was just thinking about the dinner with Montgomery…'

Darcy raised a brow. 'Yes?'

Feeling grim, Max said, 'You're coming with me.'

She straightened up at the door. 'Oh.' She looked nonplussed for a moment, and then said, 'Is that really appropriate?'

Max finally felt as if he had his recalcitrant body under some kind of control and stood up, putting his hands in his pockets. 'Yes, it's highly appropriate. You've been working on this deal with me and I'll need you there to keep track of the conversation and make nice with Montgomery's wife.'

Darcy was clearly reluctant. 'Don't you think that perhaps someone else might be more—?'

Max took one hand out of his pocket and held it up. 'I don't want any further discussion about this matter. You're coming with me—that's it.'

Darcy looked at him with those huge blue eyes and for a dizzying moment Max felt as if she could see all the way down into the depths of his being. And then the moment broke when she shrugged lightly and said, 'Okay, fine. Anything else you need this evening?'

He had a sudden vivid image of ripping her shirt open, to see her lush breasts encased in silk and satin, and got out a strangled-sounding, 'No, you can go.'

To his blessed relief, she did go. He ran both hands through his hair with frustration. Ordinarily Max would have taken this rogue reaction as a clear sign that he should go out and seek a new lover, but he knew that the last thing he needed right now in the run-up to the final negotiations with Montgomery was for him to be at the centre of headlines speculating about his colourful love-life.

So for now he was stuck in the throes of lusting after his very capable PA—an impossible situation that Max felt some god somewhere had engineered just for his own amusement.

CHAPTER TWO

A WEEK LATER Darcy was still mulling over the prospect of going to the Montgomery dinner the following evening with Max. She assured herself again that she was being ridiculous to feel so reluctant. Lots of PAs accompanied their bosses on social occasions that blurred into work.

So why was it that her pulse seemed to step up a gear when she thought about being out in public with Max, in a social environment?

Because she was an idiot. She scowled at herself and almost jumped out of her skin when Max yelled her name from inside his office. If anything, his curtness over the last week should have eased her concerns. He certainly wasn't giving her the remotest indication that there was anything but business on his mind.

She got up and hurried into his office, schooling her face into a neutral expression. As always, though, as soon as she laid eyes on him her insides clenched in reaction.

He was pacing back and forth, angry energy sparking. She sighed inwardly. This protracted deal was starting to wear on *her* nerves too.

She sat down and waited patiently, and then Max rounded on her and glared at her so fiercely her eyes widened with reproach. 'What did I do?'

He snapped his gaze away and bit out, 'Nothing. It's not you. It's—'

'Montgomery,' Darcy said flatly.

He looked at her again and his silence told her succintly that that was exactly what it was.

'I'll need you to work late this evening. I want to make sure that when we meet him tomorrow I'm not giving him one single reason to doubt my ability.'

Darcy shrugged. 'Sure thing.'

Max put his hands on his hips, a look of determination stamped on his gorgeous features. 'Okay, clear the schedule of anything else today and let's take out everything to do with this deal. I want to go through it all with a fine-tooth comb.'

Darcy got up and mentally braced herself for a gruelling day ahead.

* * *

Much later that evening Darcy sat back on her heels in Max's office and arched her spine, with her hands on the small of her back. Her shoes had come off hours ago and they'd eaten take-out.

It had to be close to midnight when Max finally said wearily, 'That's it, isn't it? We've been through every file, memo and e-mail. Checked into the man's entire history and all his business endeavours.'

Darcy smiled wryly and reached up to tuck some escaping hair back into her chignon. 'I think it's safe to say that we could write an authorised biography on Cecil Montgomery now.'

The dark night outside made Max's office feel like a cocoon. They were surrounded by the soft glow of numerous lights. He didn't respond and she looked up at him where he stood behind his desk, shirt open at the throat and sleeves rolled up. In spite of that he barely looked rumpled—whereas she felt as if she'd been dragged through a hedge backwards and was in dire need of a long, relaxing bath.

He was looking at her with a strange expression, as if caught for a moment, and it made Darcy's pulse skip. She felt self-conscious, aware of how she'd just been stretching like a cat. But then the moment passed and he moved and went over to the bar, his loose-limbed grace evident even after the day's hard slog. Darcy envied him. As *she* stood up her bones and joints protested. She told herself she was being ridiculous to imagine that Max was looking at her any kind of which way.

He came back and handed her a tumbler of dark golden liquid. Her first thought was that it was like his eyes, and then he said with a wry smile, 'Scottish whisky—I feel it's appropriate.' He was referring to Montgomery's nationality.

Darcy smiled too and clinked her glass off Max's. 'Sláinte.'

Their eyes held as they took a sip of their drinks and it was like liquid fire going down her throat. Aware that they were most likely alone in the vast building, and feeling self-consciousness again, Darcy broke the contact and moved away to sit on the edge of a couch near Max's desk.

She watched as he came and stood at the window near her, saw the scar on the his face snaking down from his temple to his jaw.

She found herself asking impulsively, 'The scar—how did you get it?'

Max tensed, and there was an almost imperceptible tightening of his fingers around his glass. His mouth thinned and he didn't look at her. 'Amazing how a scar fascinates so many people—especially women.'

Immediately Darcy tensed, feeling acutely exposed. She said stiffly, 'Sorry, it's none of my business.'

He looked at her. 'No, it's not.'

Max took in Darcy's wide eyes and a memory rushed back at him with such force that it almost felled him: a much younger Darcy, but with the same pale heart-shaped face. Concerned. Pushing between him and the boys who had been punching the breath out of him with brute force.

He'd been gasping like a grounded fish, eyes streaming, familiar humiliation and impotent anger burning in his belly, and she'd stood there like a tiny fierce virago. When they'd left and he'd got his breath back she'd turned to him, worried.

Without even thinking about what he was doing, still dizzy, Max had straightened and reached out to touch her jaw. He'd said, almost to himself, '"Though she be but little, she is fierce."'

She'd blushed and whirled around and left. He'd still been reeling from the attack—reeling from whatever impulse had led him to quote Shakespeare.

Darcy was reaching across to put her glass on the table now, standing up, clearly intending to leave. And why wouldn't she after he'd just shut her down?

An impulse rose up within Max and he heard himself say gruffly, 'It happened on the streets. Here in Rome, when I was homeless.'

Darcy stopped. She lifted her hand from the glass and looked at him warily. 'Homeless?'

Max leaned his shoulder against the solid glass window, careful to keep his face expressionless. Curiously, he didn't feel any sense of regret for letting that slip out. He nodded. 'I was homeless for a couple of years after I was kicked out of Boissy.'

Darcy said, 'I remember the blood on the snow.'

Max felt slightly sick. *He* still remembered the vivid stain of blood on the snow, and woke sometimes at night sweating. He'd vowed ever since then not to allow anyone to make him lose control again. He would beat them at their own game, in their own rareified world.

'A boy went to hospital unconscious because of me.'

She shook her head faintly. 'Why did they torment you so much?'

Max's mouth twisted. 'Because one of their fathers was my mother's current lover and he was paying my fees. They didn't take kindly to that.'

Darcy had one very vague memory of an incredibly beautiful and glamorous woman arriving at the school one year with Max, in a chauffeur-driven car.

She found herself resting against the edge of the desk, not leaving as she'd intended to moments ago. 'Why were you homeless?'

Max's face was harsh in the low light. 'My mother failed to inform me that she'd decided to move to the States with a new lover and left no forwarding details. Let's just say she wasn't exactly at the nurturing end on the scale of motherhood.'

Darcy frowned. 'You must have had other family... Your father?'

Max's face was so expressionless that Darcy had to repress a shiver.

'I have a brother, but my father died some years ago. I couldn't go to them, in any case. My father had made it clear I was my mother's responsibillty when they divorced and he wanted nothing to do with me. They lived in Brazil.'

Darcy tried not to look too shocked. 'But you must have been just—'

'Seventeen,' Max offered grimly.

'And the scar…?' It seemed to stand out even more lividly now, and Darcy had to curb the urge to reach out and touch it.

Max looked down at his drink, swirling it in his glass. 'I saw a man being robbed and chased after the guy.' He looked up again. 'I didn't realise he was a junkie with a knife until he turned around and lunged at me, cutting my face. I managed to take the briefcase from him. I won't lie—there was a moment when I almost ran with it myself… But I didn't.'

Max shrugged, as if chasing junkies and staying on the right side of his conscience was nothing.

'The owner was so grateful when I returned it

that he insisted on taking me to the hospital. He talked to me, figured out a little of my story. It turned out that he was CEO of a private equity finance firm, and as a gesture of goodwill for returning his property he offered me a position as an intern. I knew this was a chance and I vowed not to mess it up...'

Darcy said, a little wryly, 'I think it's safe to say you didn't waste the opportunity. He must have been a special man to do that.'

'He was,' Max said with uncharacteristic softness. 'One of the few people I trusted completely. He died a couple of years ago.'

There was only the faintest low hum of traffic coming from the streets far below. Isolated siren calls that faded into the distance. Everything around them was dark and golden. Darcy felt as if she were suspended in a dream. She'd never in a million years thought she might have a conversation like this with Max, who was unreadable on the best of days and never spoke of his personal life.

'You don't trust easily, then?'

Max grimaced slightly. 'I learnt early to take

care of myself. Trust someone and you make yourself weak.'

'That's so cynical,' Darcy said, but it came out flat, not with the mocking edge she'd aimed for.

Max straightened up from the window and was suddenly much closer to Darcy. She could smell him—a light tangy musk, with undertones of something much more earthy and masculine.

He looked at her assessingly. 'What about you, Darcy? Are you telling me *you're not* cynical after your parents' divorce?'

She immediately avoided that incisive gaze and looked out at the glittering cityscape beyond Max. A part of her had broken when her world had been upended and she'd been split between her parents. But as a rule it wasn't something she liked to dwell on. She was reluctant to explore the fact that it had a lot to do with her subsequent avoidance of relationships.

She finally looked back to Max, forcing her voice to sound light. 'I prefer to say realistic. Not cynical.'

The corner of Max's mouth twitched. Had he moved even closer? He felt very close to Darcy.

He drawled now, 'Let's agree to call it realistic cynicism, then. So—no dreams of a picturesque house and a white picket fence with two point two kids to repair the damage your parents did to you?'

Darcy sucked in a breath at Max's unwitting perspicacity. Damn him for once again effortlessly honing in on her weak spot: her desire to have a base. A home of her own. Not the cynical picture he painted, but her own oasis in a life that she knew well could be upended without any warning, leaving her reeling with no sense of a safe centre.

Her career had become her centre, but Darcy knew she needed something more tangibly rooted.

She tried to sound as if he hadn't hit a raw nerve. 'Do I *really* strike you as someone who is yearning for the domestic idyll?'

He shook his head and took a step closer, reaching past Darcy to put his glass on the table behind her. She knew this should feel a little weird—after all they'd never been so physically close before, beyond their handshake when she'd taken the job. But after the intensity of their day spent cocooned in this office, with the darkness outside now, and after Max had revealed the origin of his scar, a dangerous sense of familiarity suppressed Darcy's normal impulse to observe the proper boundaries.

She told herself it was their shared experience in Boissy that made things a little different than the usual normal boss/PA relationship. But really the truth was that she didn't *want* to move as Max's arm lightly brushed against hers when he straightened again. The sip of whisky she'd taken seemed to be spreading throughout her body, oozing warmth and a sense of delicious lethargy.

Max looked at her. He was so close now that she could see how his eyelashes were dark gold, lighter at the tips.

'No,' he said. 'I don't think you are looking for the domestic idyll. You strike me as someone who is very focused on her career. A bit of a loner, perhaps?'

That stung. Darcy had friends, but she'd been working away so much that she only saw them if she went back to the UK. He was right, though, and that was why it stung. The revelation that she might be avoiding platonic as well as romantic relationships was not welcome.

She cursed herself. She was allowing fatigue, a sip of whisky and some unexpected revelations from Max to seriously impair her judgement. There was no intimacy here. They were both exhausted.

She straightened up, not liking the way that put her even closer to Max. She looked anywhere but at him. 'It's late. I should get going if you want me to be awake enough to pay attention at dinner tomorrow evening.'

'Yes,' Max said. 'That's probably wise.'

Her feet seemed to be welded to the floor, but Darcy forced herself to move and turned to walk away—bumping straight into the corner of the desk, jarring her hip bone. She gave a pained gasp.

Max's hand came to her arm. 'Are you okay?'

Darcy could feel the imprint of Max's fingers, strong and firm, and just like that she was breathless. He turned her towards him and she couldn't evade his gaze.

'I... Thanks. It was nothing.' Any pain was fast being eclipsed by the look in Max's eyes.

Darcy's insides swooped and flipped. The air between them was suddenly charged in a way that made her think of running in the opposite direction. Curiously, though, she didn't want to obey this impulse.

And then something resolute crossed his face and he pulled her towards him.

Darcy was vaguely aware that Max's grip on her arm wasn't so tight that she couldn't pull free. But a sense of shock mixed with intense excitement gripped her.

'What are you doing?' she half whispered.

His gaze moved from her mouth up to her eyes and time stood still. Max's other hand moved around to the back of her neck, tugging her inexorably towards him. His voice was low and seductive. 'I haven't been able to stop thinking about what this would be like.'

'What *what* would be like?'

'This...'

Before Darcy's brain could catch up with the speed at which things were moving Max's mouth came down and covered hers, fitting to her softer contours like a jigsaw piece slotting into place.

He was hard and firm, masterful as he moved

his mouth against hers, enticing her to open up to him—which she found herself doing unhesitatingly. The kiss instantly became something else...something much deeper and darker.

Max was bold, his tongue exploring the depths of her mouth, stroking sensuously, making her lower body clench in helpless reaction. His body was whipcord-hard against hers, calling to her innermost feminine instincts that relished such evidence of his masculinity.

The edge of the desk was digging into Darcy's buttocks, but she barely noticed as Max urged her back so that she was sitting on it, moving his body between her legs so she had to widen them.

It was as if he'd simply inserted himself like a sharp blade under her skin and she'd been rendered powerless to think coherently or do anything except respond to the feverish call of her blood to taste this man, drink him in. It was intoxicating, heady, and completely out of character for her to behave like this.

Max's hands were moving now, sliding down the back of her silk shirt, resting on her waist over the belt of her trousers. And then he moved even closer between her legs and Darcy felt the thrust of his erection against her belly.

It was that very stark evidence of just how far over the edge they were tipping that blasted some cold air through the heat haze clouding her brain.

Darcy pulled back to find two slumberous pools of tawny gold staring at her. Their breathing was laboured and she was aware of thinking with sudden clarity: *Max Fonseca Roselli can't possibly want me. I'm not remotely his type. He's playing with me.*

She jerked back out of his arms and off the desk so abruptly that she surprised him into letting her go. Her heart was racing as if she'd just run half a marathon.

Some space and air between them brought Darcy back to full shaming reality. One minute they'd been knee-deep in the minutiae of Montgomery's life and business strategies, and the next she'd been sipping fine whisky and Max had been telling her stuff she'd never expected to hear.

And then she'd been climbing him like a monkey.

She'd never behaved so unprofessionally in

her life. She lambasted herself, and ignored the screeching of every nerve-end that begged her to throw herself back into his arms.

Max looked every inch the disreputable play-boy at that moment, with frustration stamped onto hard features as he observed his prey stand-ing at several feet's distance. His cheeks were slashed with colour, his hair messy. *Oh, God.* She'd had her hands in his hair, clutching him to her like some kind of sex-starved groupie.

When she felt she could speak she said accus-ingly, '*That* should not have happened.'

Her hair was coming down from its chignon and she lifted her hands to do a repair job. The fact that Max's gaze dropped to her breasts made her feel even more humiliated. If they hadn't stopped when they had— She shut her mind down from contemplating where exactly she might be right now.

Allowing him to make love to her on his desk? Like some bad porn movie cliché: Darcy Does Her Boss.

She felt sick and took her hands down now her hair was secured.

Max looked at her and didn't seem to share half

the turmoil she felt as he drawled, with irritating insouciance, '*That* did happen, and it was going to happen sooner or later.'

'Don't be ridiculous,' Darcy snapped on a panicked reflex at the thought that he had somehow seen something of her fascination with him. She was aghast to note that her legs were shaking slightly. 'You don't want me.'

Max folded his arms across his broad chest. 'I'm not in the habit of kissing women I don't want, Darcy.'

'Ha!' she commented acerbically as she started to hunt for her discarded shoes. She sent him a quick glare. 'You really expect me to believe you want *me*? That was nothing but a momentary glitch in our synapses, fuelled by fatigue and proximity.' She finally spotted her shoes and shoved her feet into them, saying curtly, 'This shouldn't have happened. It's completely inappropriate.'

'Fatigue and proximity?'

Max's scathing tone stopped Darcy in her tracks and she looked at him with the utmost reluctance. He was disgusted.

'That was chemistry—pure and simple. We

wanted each other and, believe me, if we'd been wide awake and separated by a thick stone wall I'd still have wanted you.'

Darcy's heart pounded in the explosive silence left by his words. *He wanted her?* No way. She shook her head. Panic clutched her. 'I'll hand in my notice first thing—'

'You'll do no such thing!'

Darcy's heart was pounding out of control now. 'But we can't possibly work together after this.' She crossed her arms tightly. 'You have issues with PAs who don't know their place.'

He scowled. 'What just happened was entirely mutual. I have no issue with that—it was as much my responsibility as yours. More so, in fact, as I'm your boss.'

'Exactly,' Darcy pointed out, exasperated. 'All the more reason why I can't keep working for you. We just crossed the line.'

Max knew on some rational level that everything Darcy was saying was true. He'd never lost control so spectacularly. He was no paragon of virtue, but he'd never mixed business with pleasure before, always keeping the two worlds very separate.

In all honesty he was still reeling a little from the fact that he'd so blithely allowed it to happen. And then his conscience mocked him. As if he'd had a choice. He'd been like a dog in heat—kissing Darcy had been a compulsion he'd been incapable of ignoring.

All day he'd been aware of her in a way that told him the feeling of desire that had sneaked up on him wasn't some mad aberration. As soon as she'd arrived for work he'd wanted to undo that glossy chignon and taste her lush mouth. All day he'd struggled with relegating her back to her appropriate position, telling himself he was being ridiculous.

Then they'd ordered takeout and she'd sat cross-legged on the floor, eating sushi out of a carton with chopsticks, and he'd found it more alluring than if they'd been in the glittering surroundings of a Michelin-starred restaurant. And when she'd taken her shoes off earlier and knelt down on the floor, to spread papers out and make it easier to sort them, he'd had to battle the urge to stride over and kneel down behind her, pulling her hips back—

Dio.

And now she was going to resign—because of *his* lack of control. Max's gut tightened.

'You're not walking away from this job, Darcy.'

She blinked, and a mutinous look came over her face. Her mouth was slightly swollen and Max was distracted by the memory of how soft it had felt under his. The sweet yet sharp stroke of her tongue against his… *Maledizione*. Just the thought of it was enough to fire him up all over again.

Darcy was cool. 'I don't think you have much choice in the matter.'

A familiar sense of ruthlessness coursed through Max and he reacted to her cool tone even when he felt nothing but heat. 'I do—if you care about your future job prospects.'

Darcy paled and a very unfamiliar stab of remorse caught at Max. He pushed it aside.

'I will not remain in a job where the lines of professionalism have been breached.'

Feeling slightly desperate, and not liking it, Max said again, 'It was just a kiss, Darcy.' He ran a hand impatiently through his hair. 'You're right, it shouldn't have happened, but it did.'

He thought of something else and realised with

a jolt that he'd lost track of his priorities for a moment.

'I need you to help me close this deal with Montgomery. I can't afford the upheaval a new PA will bring at the moment.'

Max saw Darcy bite her lip, small white teeth sinking into soft pink flesh. For a wild second he almost changed his mind and blurted out that maybe she was right—they'd crossed a line and she should leave—but something stopped him. He told himself it was the importance of the deal.

She turned around and paced over to the window and looked out, her back to him. Max found his gaze travelling down over that tiny waist. Her shirt was untucked, dishevelled. *He'd* done that. He could remember how badly he'd wanted to touch her skin, see if it was as silky as he imagined it would be.

The knowledge hit him starkly: the most beautiful women in the world had treated him to personal erotic strip shows and yet Max was more turned on right now by an untucked piece of faux silk chainstore shirt.

And then Darcy turned around. Her voice was low. 'I know how important this deal is to you.'

The way she said it made Max feel exposed. She couldn't know the real extent of why it was so important—that it would bring him to a place of acceptance, both internally and externally, where he would finally be able to move on from the sense of exposure and humiliation that had dogged him his whole life. And, worse, the sense of being abandoned.

Yet he couldn't deny it. 'Yes. It's important to me.'

She fixed her wide blue gaze on him but he could see how pinched her face was. Reluctance oozed from her every pore.

'I'll stay on—but only until the deal is done and only if what happened tonight doesn't happen again.'

She looked at him, waiting for a response. The truth was that if Max wanted something he got it. And he wanted Darcy. But for the first time in his life he had to recognise that perhaps he couldn't always get what he wanted. That some things were more important than others. And this deal with Montgomery was more important than having Darcy in his bed, sating his clawing sense of frustration.

Also, he didn't want her to see that it was a struggle for him to back off. That would be far too exposing.

So he said, with an easiness that belied every bone in his body that wanted to throw her onto the nearest flat surface, 'It won't happen again, Darcy. Go home. We've got another long day and evening ahead of us tomorrow. Don't forget to bring a change of clothes for dinner tomorrow night. We'll be going straight from the office.'

Darcy didn't say anything. She just turned and walked out of the room and the door closed with incongruous softness behind her.

Max walked over to the window. After a few minutes' delay he saw her emerge from the building in her coat, walking briskly away from the building, merging with Rome's late-night pedestrian traffic.

Something in his body eased slightly now that she was no longer in front of him, with those wide blue eyes looking so directly at him that he felt as if he were under a spotlight.

No woman was worth messing up this deal and certainly not little Darcy Lennox, with her provocative curves. Max finally turned around again and sighed deeply when he saw the slew of papers strewn across his desk and floor.

Instead of leaving himself, he went back to the bar, refilled his glass with whisky and then sat down and pulled the nearest sheaf of papers towards him. He put Darcy firmly out of his head.

Darcy tossed and turned in bed a little later, too wired to sleep. It was as if her body had been plugged into an electrical socket and she now had an excess of energy fizzing in her system.

She'd been plugged into Max.

Even though she was lying down, her limbs took on a jelly-like sensation when she recalled that moment of suspended tension just before he'd kissed her and everything had gone hazy and hot. She could still feel the imprint of his body against hers and between her legs she tingled. She clamped her thighs together.

They'd taken a quantum leap away from boss/PA, and it had happened so fast it still felt unreal. Had she really threatened to leave her job? And had he more or less threatened her future employment prospects if she did? She shivered slightly. She could well imagine Max doing just that—she'd witnessed his ruthlessness when it came to business associates first-hand.

The deal with Montgomery meant more to him than the potential awkwardness of having shared an intimate and highly inappropriate moment with his PA.

No matter what Max said, Darcy had no doubts that what had happened had been borne out of insanity brought on by fatigue and the moment of intimacy that had sprung up when he'd told her about his past.

She hadn't expected to hear him reveal that he'd been homeless. Any other student from Boissy wouldn't have lasted two days on the streets. But Max had lasted two years, and crawled his way out of it spectacularly.

He'd mentioned a brother, and his father. His parents' divorce. Questions resounded in Darcy's head as the enigmatic figure of Maximiliano Fonseca Roselli suddenly took on a much deeper aspect.

Unable to help herself, she leaned over and switched on the bedside light, picked up her tablet. She searched the internet for 'Max Fonseca Roselli family' and a clutch of pictures sprang up.

Darcy's breath was suspended as she scrolled through them. There was a picture of a very tall and darkly handsome man: Luca Fonseca, Brazilian industrialist and philanthropist. Max's brother. His name rang a bell. And then more pictures popped up of the same man with a stunningly beautiful blonde woman. They were wedding photos. Darcy recalled that she'd read about the wedding between Luca Fonseca and the infamous Italian socialite Serena DePiero recently.

Had Max gone to the wedding? Darcy was about to search for more information on his parents when she realised what she was doing and closed the cover of her tablet with force.

She flipped off the light and lay down, angry with herself for giving in to curiosity about a man with whom she'd shared a very brief and ill-advised moment of pure unprofessional madness. A man she should have no further interest in beyond helping him to get this deal so that she could get the hell out of his orbit and get on with her life.

CHAPTER THREE

DARCY LOOKED AT herself critically in the mirror of the ladies' toilet next to her office, but she didn't really see her own reflection. She was on edge after a long day in which Max had been overly polite and solicitous, with not so much as a sly look or hint that they'd almost made love on his desk the previous night.

At one stage she'd nearly snapped at him to please go back to normal and snarl at her the way he usually did.

The fact that she'd allowed a level of exposure and intimacy with Max she'd never allowed before was something she was resolutely ignoring. Her previous sexual experiences with men had come only after a lengthy dating period. And in each case once the final intimacy had been breached she'd backed off, because she'd realised she had no desire to deepen the commitment.

She snorted at herself now. As if she would have to worry about something like that with Max Fonseca Roselli. He was the kind of man who would leave so fast your head would be spinning for a week.

She forced her mind away from Max and took a deep breath. Her dress was black and had been bought for exactly this purpose—to go from work to a social event. And, as far as Darcy had been concerned when she'd bought it, it was modest.

Yet now it felt all wrong. It was a dress that suited her diminutive hourglass shape perfectly, but suddenly the scooped neckline was too low and the waist too cinched in. The clingy fabric was a little *too* clingy around her bottom and thighs, making her want to pluck it away from her body. The capped sleeves felt dressy, and when she moved the discreet slit up one side seemed to shout out, *I'm trying to be sexy!*

All at once she felt pressured and frazzled, aware of time ticking on. She'd already been in the bathroom for twenty minutes. She imagined Max pacing up and down outside, looking at his watch impatiently, waiting for her. Well, too late to change now. Darcy refreshed her make-up and spritzed on some perfume, and slid her feet into slightly higher heels than normal.

She'd left her hair down and at the last moment felt a lurch of panic when she looked at herself again. It looked way too undone. She twisted it up into a quick knot and secured it with a pin.

Her cheeks were hot and beads of sweat rolled down between her breasts. Cursing Max, and herself, she finally let herself out, her work clothes folded into a bag. It was with some relief that she noted that Max wasn't pacing up and down outside.

Stowing her bag in a cupboard, making a mental note to take it home after the weekend, Darcy took a deep breath and knocked once briefly on Max's office door before going in.

When she did, though, she nearly took a step back. Max was standing with a remote control in his hand, watching a financial news channel on the flat screen TV set into his wall. His hair was typically messy, but otherwise any resemblance to the Max she'd expected to see dissolved into a haze of heat.

His jaw was clean-shaven, drawing the eye to strong, masculine lines. He was wearing a classic three-piece suit in dark grey, with a snowy-white shirt and grey silk tie. Darcy swallowed as Max turned and his gaze fell on her. She couldn't breathe. Literally couldn't draw breath. She'd never seen anyone so arrestingly gorgeous in her life. And the memory of how that lean body had felt when it was pressed against hers, between her legs, was vivid enough to make her sway slightly.

There was a long, taut silence between them until Max clicked a button on the remote and the faint hum of chatter from the TV stopped.

He arched a brow. 'Ready?'

Darcy found her voice. 'Yes.'

He moved towards her and she backed out of his office, almost tripping over her own feet to pick up her evening bag and a light jacket matching the dress. As she struggled into it inelegantly she felt it being held out for her and muttered embarrassed thanks as Max settled it onto her shoulders.

She cursed the imagination that made her think his fingers had brushed suggestively against the back of her neck, and strode out of the office ahead of Max before she could start thinking anything else. Like how damn clingy her dress felt right then, and what rogue devil had prompted her not to wear stockings. The slide of her bare thighs against one another felt sensual in a way she'd never even noticed before. She'd never been given to erotic flights of fancy. Far too pragmatic.

Darcy didn't look at Max as they waited for his private lift, but once they were inside his scent dominated the small space.

He asked, 'You have the documents?'

'Yes.' Darcy lifted the slim attaché case she carried alongside her bag. It held some documents they wanted to have on hand in case Montgomery asked for them.

The lift seemed to take an eternity to descend the ten or so floors to the bottom.

'You know, we *will* have to make eye contact at some point in the evening.' Max's voice was dry.

Reluctantly Darcy looked up at him, standing beside her, and it was as if a jolt of lightning zapped her right in the belly. She sucked in a breath and saw Max's eyes flare. The shift in energy was as immediate as an electric current springing up between them, as if it had been waiting until they got close enough to activate it.

No wonder they'd been skirting around each other all day. They'd both been avoiding *this*.

For the nano-second it took for this to sink in, and for Max to make an infinitesimally small move towards her—for her to realise how badly she wanted to touch him again—there was nothing outside of the small cocoon of the lift. Desire pulsated like a tangible thing.

But then a sharp *ping* sounded, the doors opened silently and they both stopped—centimetres from actually touching each other.

Max emitted a very rude Italian curse. He took her arm to guide her out of the lift, although it felt more as if he was marching her out of the building.

Once outside, walking to his chauffeur-driven car, he said tersely, 'I said eye contact, Darcy, not—'

'Not *what*, Max?' Darcy stopped and pulled her arm free, shaky from the rush of adrenalin and desire she'd just experienced, and self-conscious at the thought that she'd been all but drooling. 'I didn't do anything. *You're* the one who looked at me as if—'

He came close. 'As if *what*? As if I suddenly

couldn't think of anything else except what happened last night?' His mouth was a thin line. 'Well, I couldn't—and neither could you.'

Darcy had nothing to say. He was right. She'd been utterly naïve and clueless to think that she could experience a moment like that with Max Fonseca Roselli and put it down as a rash, crazy incident and never want him again. A hunger had been awoken inside her.

But she could deal with that.

What she couldn't deal with was the fact that Max—for some unfathomable reason—still wanted her too.

He glanced at his watch and said curtly, 'We'll be late. We can't talk about this now.'

And then he took her arm again and led her to the car, following her into the plush interior before she could protest or say another word.

The journey to the restaurant was made in a silence that crackled with electric tension. Darcy didn't look anywhere near Max, afraid of what she'd see if she did. She couldn't handle that blistering gaze right now.

One thing was clear, though. She would be

handing in her notice *before* this deal was done. She couldn't continue to work for Max after this. But she didn't think he'd appreciate hearing her tender resignation right now.

The car came to a stop outside one of Rome's most exclusive restaurants. It took lesser mortals about six months to get a table, but Max had a table whenever he wanted.

He helped her out of the car, and even though Darcy wanted to avoid physical contact as much as possible she had to take his hand or risk sprawling in an ungainly heap at his feet.

She'd just stood up straight, and Max was still holding her hand, when a genial voice came from nearby.

'You didn't mention that you were bringing a date.'

Darcy tensed, and Max's hand tightened on hers reflexively. But almost in the same second she could tell he'd recovered and his hand moved smoothly to her arm as he brought her around to meet their nemesis.

Cecil Montgomery was considerably shorter than Max, and considerably older, with almost white hair. But he oozed charisma, and Darcy was surprised to find that on first impression she liked him.

His eyes were very blue, and twinkled benignly at her, but she could see the steeliness in their depths. A tall woman stood at his side, very elegant and graceful, with an open friendly face and dark grey eyes. Her hair was silver and swept up into a classic chignon.

'Please—let me introduce you to my wife, Jocasta Montgomery.'

'Pleasure…' Darcy let her hand be engulfed, first by Montgomery's and then by his wife's.

It was only when they were walking into the restaurant that Darcy realised Max hadn't actually introduced her as his PA—or had he and she just hadn't heard?

She hadn't had anything to do with Montgomery herself, as he and Max had a direct line of communication, so it was quite possible he still thought she was Max's date. The thought made Darcy feel annoyingly self-conscious.

They left their coats in the cloakroom and were escorted to their table, the ladies walking ahead of the men. The restaurant oozed timeless luxury and exclusivity. Darcy recognised Italian politicians and a movie star. The elaborate furnishings wouldn't have been out of place in Versailles, and even the low-pitched hum of conversation was elegant.

Jocasta Montgomery took Darcy's arm and said *sotto voce* in a melodious Scottish accent, 'I don't know about you, my dear, but I always find that places like this give me an almost overwhelming urge to start flinging food around the place.'

It was so unexpected that Darcy let out a startled laugh and something inside her eased out of its tense grip. She replied, 'I know what you mean—it's an incitement to rebel.'

They arrived at a round table, the best in the room, and took their seats. To Darcy's surprise the conversation started and flowed smoothly. Max and Montgomery dominated it, with talk of current business trends and recent scandals. At one point between starters and the main course Jocasta rolled her eyes at Darcy and led her into a conversation about living in Rome and what she liked about it.

They skirted around the edges of the fact that this dinner was really about whether or not Montgomery was going to hand his precious life's blood to Max to manage until coffee had been served after dessert.

Darcy had almost forgotten why they were there, she'd enjoyed talking to Jocasta so much. But now there was a palpable buzz of tension in the air and Darcy saw the very evident steely gleam in Montgomery's eyes as he looked at Max, who was unmistakably tense.

It was slightly disconcerting to recognise how keenly she felt Max's tension as Montgomery looked at him over his coffee cup before putting it down slowly.

'The fact is, Max, quite simply there is no one I can imagine handling this fund and making it grow into the future better than you. As you're aware I'm very concerned about philanthropy, and your own brother's work has been inspirational to me.'

Max inclined his head towards the older man, but his face was expressionless.

'My one reservation, however, is this...'

Darcy tensed and avoided looking at Max.

'You have been leading a committedly single lifestyle for a long time.' He glanced at Darcy and said half apologetically, 'Present company notwithstanding. My fund and my life's work has been built upon and developed with family in mind. *My* family, primarily, of course, but also for the benefit of many others. This would never have happened if I hadn't had a very strong sense of family values running through previous generations. That's why the Montgomery fund has lasted as long as it has, and grown so strong...'

Darcy was barely aware of Montgomery's continued misunderstanding about who she was. He was going on...

'And you, Max—you come from a broken home... For years you were estranged from your father, you didn't speak to your own twin brother, and you are not close to your mother.'

Darcy's mind boggled. Max's brother was a *twin*?

She looked at him now and could see his face was still expressionless, but a vein popped slightly over one temple, near his scar, which stood out against that dark olive skin. The scar he'd got because his own mother had forgotten about him. Left him defenceless on the streets.

'You've done your research,' Max said easily,

but Darcy recognised the edge of something dangerous.

Montgomery shrugged. 'No more than you yourself have done, no doubt.'

'My relationship with my brother, my mother, has no bearing on my ability to manage your fund, Cecil.'

A lesser man would have quailed at the distinct threat in Max's voice. Not Montgomery.

'No,' said the other man, looking at Max assessingly. 'I think for the most part you are right. But my concern would be the risks you'd be prepared to take on behalf of my fund—risks that you might not consider taking if you had a different perspective on life. My fear is that, based on your experiences, you might actually be biased against the very values I've built this fund upon, and that it would influence your decision-making process because you have only yourself to worry about.'

Darcy's insides had turned to stone. Cecil Montgomery, with a ruthless precision she'd never even witnessed in Max, had just laid Max's life bare and dissected it with clinical and damning detachment.

She felt a very disturbing surge of something like protectiveness. A need to defend.

Even Jocasta Montgomery had put her hand on her husband's arm and was saying something indistinct to him.

Darcy looked at Max, who had carefully put his own coffee cup down. The restaurant was largely empty by now.

'You are right about almost everything, Cecil.' He smiled, but it was a thin, harsh line. 'I do come from a broken home, and my brother and I did suffer at the hands of two parents who really couldn't have cared less about our welfare.'

Jocasta broke in. 'Please, Max, don't feel you have to say—'

But Max held up a hand, not taking his gaze off Montgomery. 'I said that your husband is right about *almost* everything. There's one thing his research hasn't shown up, however.'

Montgomery raised a brow. 'I'm intrigued. What is it that I've missed?'

Max's jaw clenched, and to Darcy's shock he reached over and took her hand in his, holding it tight.

'Darcy.'

Darcy looked at Max, but he hadn't said her name to call her attention and speak to her.

He was still looking at Montgomery and gripping her hand tight as he said, 'You can be the first to congratulate my fiancée and I on our engagement.'

Darcy might have enjoyed Montgomery's almost bug-eyed response if she hadn't been so afraid that her own eyes were bugging out of her head at the same moment.

'But… But…' Jocasta Montgomery said, 'Darcy told me she's your PA…'

Max looked at Darcy briefly and through waves of shock she could see something implacable in his expression that forbade her from saying anything.

He looked back to the couple on the other side of the damask-covered table. 'She is. That's how we met…again.'

'Again?' asked Montgomery sharply.

Max nodded. 'Darcy and I went to the same school—Boissy le Chateau in Switzerland. That's where we first met. She came to work for me three months ago…' Max shrugged, 'And the rest, as they say, is history.'

'Oh, Cecil.' Jocasta Montgomery put her hand over her husband's and looked at him with suspiciously bright eyes. 'That's how *we* met.'

Darcy felt it like a punch to the gut. She remembered that small detail now. Jocasta had been his secretary in the seventies, in Edinburgh.

Cecil Montgomery was looking at Max through narrowed eyes. Obviously suspicious. And then he turned his gaze on Darcy and she could feel her cheeks grow hot.

'Well, then, my dear, it would seem that congratulations are in order. When did this happy event occur?'

Max's hand tightened on hers as he inserted smoothly, 'Some weeks ago…I knew after just a few weeks that Darcy was unlike any other woman I've ever known. We had a bond at school…and it was rekindled.'

Darcy was still too shocked even to consider saying anything, but she tried to pull her hand out from under Max's—to no avail.

'My dear, are you quite all right? You look a little ill.' Jocasta Montgomery was leaning forward with concern.

Darcy sensed Max's tension beside her, reaching out to envelop her, inhibit her. She knew that she should pull away, stand up, throw her napkin down and say that it was all untrue. This was her chance. She should walk away from Max right now and not look back.

And put a nail in the coffin of his chance to get this deal with Cecil Montgomery.

If she wanted revenge for what he'd just done that was what she'd do.

But she couldn't get out of her head the way Montgomery had so brutally assessed Max's background, casting doubts on his ability. And she couldn't get out of her head the way she'd felt that instinctive need to defend him. And right now the instinct was still there, in spite of the rage bubbling down low at having been put in this untenable position.

She forced a smile and looked at Jocasta. 'I'm fine—really. It's just a bit of a shock to hear it made official. Up till now it's been our secret.'

She risked a glance at Max and her gaze was caught and snared by his. It was expressionless, but something flickered in the depths of those extraordinary eyes. *Relief?* His hand loosened on hers fractionally.

Jocasta was making a *tsk*ing noise. 'And my husband provoked Max into letting it slip? Well, I think the least we can do is celebrate now that your secret is out.'

Before Darcy could say anything else a waiter was summoned and a bottle of vintage champagne was being delivered to the table and expertly poured into slim flutes. It seemed to Darcy that everything was moving at warp speed, and her heart was beating too fast.

They were all holding up their glasses and Jocasta was beaming at them. Her husband was still looking less than convinced though and Max's jaw was tight. Darcy felt an urge to giggle, and quickly took a sip of the sparkling drink to make it go down.

'When are you getting married?'

Darcy looked at Montgomery, just as Max said, with all the natural-born charm of a ruthless man intent on his prize, 'Two weeks.'

His hand tightened on Darcy's again and when she turned to him he looked at her so intently that her insides combusted.

'I want to make her mine before she realises what I'm really like and leaves me for ever.'

For the first time since Max had made his outrageous statement Darcy felt her wits return. She pulled her hand free and said with some acerbity, while holding up her hand, 'Well, seeing as you haven't even bought me a ring yet, *darling*, I'm thinking that perhaps there's a flaw in the arrangements.'

Jocasta chuckled. 'Yes, Max, a lady in possession of a marriage proposal generally deserves a beautiful ring.'

Max smiled, and it was dangerous. He took Darcy's hand again and lifted it to his mouth, pressing a kiss over her ring finger, making any of the wits that had come back to her melt again.

'Which is why I've arranged to take my fiancée to Paris tomorrow, for a private appointment in Devilliers—it was meant to be a surprise.'

Darcy's eyes opened wide. Devilliers was possibly the oldest and most exclusive jewellers in the world.

Jocasta made a noise. 'And now we've ruined it. Cecil, stop goading Max. They're engaged. Look at them—they can't keep their eyes off each other.'

'Well, then,' said the older man. 'It seems that

perhaps your perspective is indeed changing, Max. However, I've decided that the announcement of my decision as to whom I'm entrusting my fund will take place at our fortieth wedding anniversary celebrations in Scotland, surrounded by my family.'

The Montgomerys shared a fond look and Max let Darcy's hand go. Montgomery looked at him, and then to Darcy. 'You will both, of course, be extended an invitation. It takes place in three weeks. Perhaps you could include the trip to Inverness as a detour on your honeymoon?'

Honeymoon?

The full enormity of what was occurring hit Darcy, and as if sensing her dawning horror Max put a firm hand on her leg, under the table, just above her knee.

'We would like nothing more—would we, *cara*?'

Max was looking at her, his big hand heavy on her leg, and treacherous heat was spreading upwards to between her thighs. 'No...'

Max knew exactly what Darcy's very ineffectual 'no' meant. It didn't mean that she agreed—it meant *Stop this now*. But he took ruthless advantage of the ambiguity and angled his body towards hers, slipping his other hand around the back of her bare neck, pulling her towards him so that he could cover her mouth with his and stop her from saying anything else.

By the time he let her go again she was hot, breathless, addled and completely out-manoeuvred by a master. The Montgomerys were preparing to leave, saying their goodbyes, clearly believing that they were playing gooseberry now.

Darcy didn't know if she wanted to stamp her foot, slap Max, or scream for them all to *stop* so she could put them right. But, like the treacherous heat that had licked up her thighs and into her belly during Max's kiss, something was holding her back—and she was too much of a coward to investigate what it was.

They stood to bid goodbye to the older couple and Darcy was vaguely aware that the restaurant had emptied. When they were alone again Max sat down, a look of supreme satisfaction on his face.

This time Darcy *did* throw down her napkin, and he looked at her. Anger at herself for being so weak made her blurt out, 'What the *hell* do you think you're playing at, Max?'

Max cast a quick look around and took Darcy's wrist, pulling her down. She landed heavily on the seat.

Something occurred to her then—an awful suspicion. 'Please tell me you didn't have that planned all along?'

Max's jaw firmed. He was unapologetic. 'No, but I saw an opportunity and took it.'

Darcy let out a slightly horrified laugh. 'An *opportunity*? That's what you call fabricating a fake engagement to your PA?'

He turned to face her, stretching an arm across the back of her chair, placing his other hand on the table. Boxing her in.

'It won't be a fake engagement, Darcy. We're going to get married.'

Darcy's mouth opened but nothing came out. On some level she had known what she was doing, going along with Max's crazy pronouncement, but she'd also expected that as soon as they were alone again he'd reassure her that of course it wouldn't happen. It had been just to placate

Montgomery and there would be some method of undoing what had been done.

She shook her head, as if that might restore sanity and order. But he was still looking at her.

She found her voice. 'Maybe it's the fatigue, Max, or the stress, but I think it's quite possible that you've gone entirely mad. This conversation is over and this *relationship* is over. Find someone else to be your convenient bride/PA, because I'm not going to be it just because I'm under your nose and you've decided that it's appropriate to kiss me when you feel like it. We both know I'm not your type of woman. No one will ever believe you've chosen to marry someone like me—Montgomery patently didn't believe a word of it—so in the end it'll achieve nothing.'

Darcy was breathless after the tumult of words and stood up on shaky legs. Before Max could stop her she turned to walk quickly through the restaurant, reality slamming back into her with each step. And humiliation. Max had seen an opportunity, all right—a cheap one, at Darcy's expense. To think that he would *use* her like this, just to further his own aims, shouldn't have come as a shock. But it did.

* * *

Max watched Darcy walk away, rendered uncharacteristically dumb. He could appreciate her very apparent sense of shock because he was still reeling himself, trying to recall what exactly had prompted him to make such an outrageous statement to Montgomery.

And then he remembered. *'You come from a broken home...estranged from your mother... brother...different perspective...'* He remembered the hot rush of rage when Montgomery had so coolly laid his life bare for inspection. Questioning his motives and ability based upon his experiences.

He'd wanted to do something to take that knowing smirk off Montgomery's face. And in a moment of mad clarity he'd known what he had to do to push the man off his sanctimonious perch. Fake a marriage. To Darcy.

And she'd gone along with it—even if she *had* looked as if someone had just punched her in the belly.

Darcy. Max's usual clear-headed focus came back and he went cold inside at the thought of

Darcy leaving. She wasn't going anywhere—not now. Not when everything was at stake.

'Get in the car, Darcy. Please.'

Darcy was valiantly ignoring Max and the open car door nearby. She was about to stretch her arm out to hail a passing taxi when he took her arm in a firm grip and all but manhandled her into the back of the car.

She sputtered, 'This is kidnap.'

Max was terse. 'Hardly. Take us to my apartment, please, Enzo.' And then he hit a button so that a partition went up, enclosing them in silence.

Darcy folded her arms and looked at the man on the other side of the car. In a louche sprawl of big long limbs, he'd never looked more like a rebel.

'You've gone too far this time, Max. I don't care what you have to do but we're *not* getting married—I've changed my mind, I'm not waiting until the deal is done. I'm on the first plane out of Rome as soon as you let me go.'

Max gave her a withering look. 'There's no need for dramatics. We are just going to talk.'

He leaned back and looked out of the window, clearly done with the conversation for now. Darcy fumed, hating the ever-present hum of awareness in her blood at being in such close proximity to him. He was such an arrogant...*bastard*. Saying the word, even silently, made her feel marginally better.

Within minutes they were pulling up outside a sleek modern building. Max was out of the car and holding out a hand for Darcy before she could think what to do. Knowing she couldn't escape now, she scowled and put her hand into his, let him help her out, jerking her hand away as soon as she was on her own two feet.

Max led her into a massive steel-and-chrome foyer, where huge works of modern art were hung on the walls. It was hushed and exclusive, and in spite of herself she found herself wondering what Max's apartment would be like.

With an acknowledgement to the concierge, Max led Darcy to an open lift and stabbed at the 'P' button. Of course, Darcy thought snarkily. Of *course* he'd be living in the penthouse.

Once in the lift she moved to the far corner. Max leaned back against the wall and looked at her from under hooded lids. 'No need to look like a startled rabbit, Darcy. I'm not going to eat you.'

'No,' she said sharply. 'Just turn my world upside down.'

CHAPTER FOUR

DARCY FOLLOWED MAX into his apartment warily. From what she could see, as he flicked on low lights, it was as sleek and modern as the building that housed it. Floor-to-ceiling windows offered astounding views of Rome glittering at night.

Her feet were sore in the high-heeled shoes, but she would let them bleed before taking them off. She was still recalling her bare feet in the office the previous night—the cocoon of intimacy and where that had led.

'Drink?'

Darcy looked over to where Max was pulling his tie out of its knot and undoing the top buttons of his shirt. He'd already taken off his jacket and he looked sinfully sexy in the waistcoat of the three-piece suit.

She shook her head. 'No. I don't want a drink, Max, and I don't want to talk. I'd like to go to some corner of the earth far away from you.'

He just shrugged, ignoring her pronounce-ment, and proceeded to pour himself a measure of something. He gestured to a seat. 'Please—sit down.'

Darcy clutched her bag tighter. 'I told you...I don't want to—'

'Well, tough, because we're talking.'

Darcy made a rude sound and stalked over to an uncomfortable-looking chair and sat down.

Max started to pace, then stopped and said, 'Look, I didn't plan to announce an engagement to you this evening.'

'I'm not so sure you didn't, Max. It certainly seemed to trip off your tongue very easily—along with that very inventive plan to treat me to a Devilliers ring. Tell me, are we taking your private jet?'

Max cursed before downing his drink in one and setting the glass down with a clatter.

He glared at her. 'I didn't plan it. He just... *Dio.* You heard him.'

Darcy's insides tightened as she recalled the sense of protectiveness that had arisen when Montgomery had baldly dissected Max's life. The truth was that no one goaded Max. He'd remained impervious in the face of much worse provocation. *But this had been personal. About his family.*

Darcy stood up, feeling vulnerable. 'I heard him, Max. The man clearly has strong feelings about the importance of family, but do you think he really cares if you're married or not?'

'You heard him. He believes my perspective will be skewed unless I have someone to worry about other than myself.' Max sounded bitter.

'So you fed me to him?'

He looked at her. 'Yes.'

'I'm just a means to an end—so you can get your hands on that fund.'

Max looked at Darcy. Her hair had begun to get dishevelled, falling down in tendrils around her face and neck. *'I'm just a means to an end.'* Why did those words strike at him somewhere? Of *course* she was a means to an end—everything in his life was a means to an end. And that end was in sight.

'Yes.'

Her jaw tightened and she stepped back. Max

did not like the flash of something like panic in his gut.

'Yes, you *are* a means to an end—I won't pretty it up and lie to you. But, Darcy, if you do this you won't walk away empty-handed. You can name your price.'

She let out a short curt laugh and it made Max wince inwardly. It sounded so unlike her.

'Believe me, no price could buy me as your wife, Max. I don't think I even *like* you all that much.'

Max felt that like a blow to his gut, but he gritted out, 'I'm not asking you to like me, and I'm not *buying* a wife, Darcy. I'm asking you to do this as part of your job. Admittedly it's a little above and beyond the call of duty…but you will be well compensated.'

Darcy tossed her head. 'Nothing could induce me to do this.'

'Nothing…?' Max asked silkily as he moved a little closer, his vision suddenly overwhelmed with the tantalising way Darcy filled out her dress.

She put out a hand. 'Stop right there.'

Max stopped, but his blood was still leaping.

He'd yet to meet a woman he couldn't seduce. *Was he prepared to seduce Darcy into agreement?* His mind screamed caution, but his body screamed *yes*!

He erred on the side of caution.

Darcy's hand was still held out. 'Don't even *think* about it, Max. That kiss…whatever happened between us…was a mistake and it won't be happening again.'

He kept his mouth closed even as he wanted to negate what she'd said. He needed her acquiescence now.

'Everyone has a price, Darcy. You can name yours. We only need to be married for as long as it takes the deal to be done, then we'll divorce and you can get on with your life. No harm done. It's just an extension of your job, and I'll make sure that you get a job wherever you want in the world after this.'

She snorted, telling him succintly what she thought of *that*. She moved away from him now, stalking over to one of the big windows.

Max felt disorientated for a moment. It wasn't usual for him to bring a woman back to his apartment. He preferred to keep women out of his private space. Especially women he seduced. Because he never wanted them to get any notions.

But Darcy was here, and it felt bizarrely as if she'd been here before. He was too consumed with bending her to his will right now to look at *that* little nugget. Too consumed with ignoring the inferno raging in his blood as he took in her curvy silhouette against the backdrop of Rome outside.

And then she turned around, her hands still clutching her bag. 'Why is this so important to you?'

Max immediately went still, as if drawing his energy back inwards. Darcy had a moment to collect herself, to try and remove her see-sawing emotions and hormones from this situation.

As she'd looked out of the window she'd had to ask herself why the prospect of marrying Max was such a red-hot button for her. Apart from the fact that it was a ludicrous thing to ask of anyone.

After all, she came from a *very* broken home, so if anyone had the necessary cynicsm to embark on a marriage of convenience it was her.

And she was ambitious enough to appreciate the aspect that Max wasn't exaggerating—she *would* have the pick of any job she wanted if she did this. It would be the least he owed her.

But she was not stupid enough to think that the way she'd felt when Max had kissed her could be ignored. He'd tapped into something untouched deep inside her—something that went beyond the physical to a secret place she'd never explored herself, never mind with anyone else.

And there was his astounding arrogance in thinking she would just go along with this decree. Like some king who expected his minions to obey his every word.

'Well, Max? If I'm to even consider this crazy idea for one second I want to know why you want this so badly.'

He seemed to glower at her for a long moment, and then he stuck his hands in the pockets of his trousers and came closer. Darcy couldn't move back because the window was behind her. He came and stood near her, looking out at the view, face tight.

'Montgomery mentioned my brother. We're twins. We were six when our parents split up and split *us* up. I only ever saw Luca again when he came to Rome for brief holidays or on trips to see our mother. I see him a little more frequently since we've been adults.'

Max sighed.

'He grew up being groomed to be my father's heir. There was never any question of me getting a share. That was my punishment for choosing to go with my mother…not that our father really cared which son he got as long as he had an heir to pass his corrupt legacy on to. But that's just part of it. Luca did offer me my half of his inheritance after our father died, but I didn't want it.'

He looked at Darcy then, almost accusingly.

'I didn't want his charity and I still don't. By then I'd already made my first million. I wanted to succeed on my own merit—surpass anything my father had ever done. Do it on my own. It's the one thing that's kept me going through it all. The need to know that I've done it without anyone handing me anything.'

He looked away again and Darcy was silent. Mesmerised by the passion blazing out of Max. And the unmistakable pride.

'For years I felt tainted. Tainted by my mother's lack of care and her sordid affairs. That's how she made her living—little better than women who call themselves what they really are: prostitutes.'

Darcy winced.

'I was on the streets one night, foraging for food in a bin at the back of an exclusive restaurant, when some guests came outside to smoke. Boys from my class at Boissy.'

She sucked in a breath, imagining the scene all too well.

As if he'd guessed her suspicion his mouth quirked and he said, 'There was no blood. I walked away—but not before they recognised me and told me that they'd never expected anything more of someone like me. I'd been born into one of the wealthiest families in South America, but thanks to my fickle parents my brother and I were used almost like an experiment to see who would flourish better. One of us was given everything. The other one had everything stripped away.'

He turned to look at her, his face stark in the dim lights.

'That's why I want this. Because if Montgomery hands me his fund I'll have proved that even when you have your birthright stripped away it's still possible to regain your dignity and get respect.'

He didn't have to elaborate for Darcy to imagine how his litany of humiliations had bred the proud man in front of her. Montgomery held an almost mythical place in the world's finances. Akin to financial royalty. Darcy knew that what Max said was true. His endorsement would make Max untouchable, revered. The boys who had bullied him at school and witnessed him at his lowest moment on the streets would be forced to respect him.

'And it's not just for me,' he said now, interrupting her thoughts. 'I'm a partner in a philanthropic organisation with my brother. We're finally putting our father's corrupt legacy to good use, and I'll be damned if I can't contribute my own share.'

Max turned to face her more fully.

'*That's* why I want this, Darcy. Everyone has a price. I've just told you mine. You can name yours.'

Why did that sound like the worst kind of deal with the devil?

Because it is, whispered a small voice.

When Darcy woke up the next day she felt strangely calm. As if a storm had passed and she'd been washed up on land—alive and breathing, if a little battered.

Max had made no further attempt to stop her from leaving once she'd said, 'I need a night to think it over.'

It was as if he'd recognised how precarious his chance was. He'd escorted her down to his car and bade her goodnight, saying, 'Just think of your price, Darcy.'

And so she had.

After hours of tossing and turning she'd got up and looked at her tablet, at the properties she'd marked on a website. It was her secret, most favourite thing to do. Earmark the properties she'd buy if she had the money.

Her heart had thumped hard when she'd seen that her current favourite was still available. The price, in her eyes, was extortionate; London property gone mad. But she knew to Max it would be a pittance. Was *this* her price? A place of her own? The base she wanted so badly? The base it would take her years to afford under normal working circumstances?

Darcy could empathise with Max's determination to do it all on his own. She could ask her parents for the money to buy a house and have it tomorrow. But when she'd seen her father almost lose everything it had forged in her a deep desire to ensure her own financial stability, to be dependent on no one else.

She'd been eight when her parents had split up and she'd been tossed back and forth like a rag doll, across time zones and countries, with nice airline ladies holding her hand through airports. It had been in those moments that Darcy had wished most fervently that she still had a home—somewhere she could go back to that would always be there. *Something that wasn't in a constant state of flux*. Security. Stability.

When Max had revealed that he'd been only six when his parents had split up her silly heart had constricted. And he had a twin brother. She couldn't imagine what it must have been like to have been ripped apart from a sibling. Never mind taken to the other side of the world, never to connect with one of your parents again.

She got up and showered and made herself coffee. She hated that knowing about Max's tumultuous past made it harder for her to keep seeing him as ruthless and cynical. But he *was*, she assured herself. Nothing had changed. He was out for himself—unashamedly. And yet who could blame him? He'd been abandoned by his own mother, forgotten by his father. Estranged from his brother.

The thing was, did he deserve for her to help him?

Darcy's mobile phone pinged with a text message. From Max.

Well?

She almost smiled. Something about his obvious impatience at the fact that she wouldn't come to heel easily comforted her. Things had morphed from relatively normal to seriously weird in a very short space of time.

She texted back.

Do you think you could use that word in a sentence?

She pictured him scowling. A couple of minutes passed and then…

Dear Darcy,
Please will you marry me so that I can secure Montgomery's fund and live happily ever after? Yours truly, Max.

Darcy barked out a laugh. The man was truly a bastard. Her phone pinged again.

Well?

Now *she* scowled.

I'm thinking.

Think faster.

Darcy threw her phone down for a moment. Pressure was building in her chest. And then the picture of the property she loved so much caught her eye. If she did this, she would get that.

We all have a price.

She picked up the phone, almost daring it to ping again with some terse message—because if it did she would tell Max where to go. But it didn't, almost as if he knew how close she was to saying no.

She took a deep breath and texted.

If—and that's a big if—if I agree to do this I want £345,000.

She let out a breath, feeling like a mercenary bitch. But it was the price of the flat she loved. And if she was being a mercenary bitch she was nothing in comparison to Max. His soul was black.

She continued.

Also, this farcical marriage will last only for as long as it takes Montgomery to announce his decision, and then you will give me a stunning reference which will open the door to whatever job I want.

Her heart thumped hard as she looked over the text, and then her finger pressed the 'Send' button. 'Delivered' appeared almost straight away.

It took longer than she'd expected, but finally Max's response came back.

Done and done. Whatever you want. I told you. Now, what's it to be?

Darcy's finger traced over the picture of the flat. In a few months she could be living there, with a new job. A new start. A settled existence for the first time since she'd been a child. And no Max messing with her hormones and her ability to think clearly.

She texted quickly before she lost her nerve: Yes.

Almost immediately a message came back.

Good. My car will pick you up in an hour. We're going to Paris.

The ring. For a moment Darcy almost texted Max back, saying she'd changed her mind, but her fingers hovered ineffectually over her phone. And then she got distracted.

What the hell did someone wear on a whirlwind trip to Paris to buy an engagement ring for a fake wedding?

* * *

In the end Darcy decided to wear one of her smarter work outfits: a dark navy wrap dress with matching high heels. She felt self-conscious now, in the small plane, and resisted the urge to check and see if her dress was gaping a little too much. The way Max had looked at her when she'd walked out of her apartment building had almost made her turn around and change into jeans and a T-shirt.

He was dressed similarly, smart/casual in a dark blue suit and white shirt. When she'd walked over to the car earlier he'd smirked slightly and said, 'We're matching—isn't that cute?'

Darcy had scowled and dived into the car. When he'd joined her she'd said, 'Can you put up the partition, please?'

She'd been more discomfited than she'd liked to admit by this more unreadable and yet curiously accessible Max. The boundary lines had become so blurred now they were non-existent, and she'd needed to lay down some rules.

When the window had gone up she'd crossed her arms over her chest. Max's eyeline had dropped to her cleavage.

'We need to discuss some formalities.'

Max's eyes had snapped up. 'Formalities?'

'All this marriage is, as far as I'm concerned, is a serious amount of overtime. You're basically paying me to be an executive PA par excellence. It's still just *work*. And if I hadn't agreed to this I would still be tendering my notice because of what happened the other night.'

Max sat back, looking dangerous and sexy, jaw dark with stubble. 'What happened, Darcy?'

Darcy shot a look at the partition and back again, her cheeks growing hot. 'You know very well what happened. We crossed the line.'

'We almost made love on my desk.'

Darcy felt hotter. 'But we didn't.' *Thank God.* 'We came to our senses.' She waved a hand. 'What I'm trying to say is that even now we are embarking on this ridiculous charade—'

'That I'll be paying you handsomely for...' Max pointed out, immediately making Darcy's irritation levels rise.

'And for which you'll be earning your place among the financial giants of the world,' she lashed back.

Max's jaw clenched. 'Touché.'

Darcy had leaned forward in her agitation but she pulled back now, forcing herself to stay calm. 'What I'm saying is that this marriage is going to be fake in every sense of the word. If you want anything physical then I'm sure you can get it from the legion of women in your little black book.'

Max folded his arms and regarded her. 'There's something incredibly ironic about the fact that I always swore I'd never enter into the state of matrimony and yet now I find myself on the brink of such a situation—'

'Caused by *you*,' Darcy flung at him.

That made him dip his head in acknowledgement before he continued, 'I find myself with a wife who won't sleep with me. I would never have anticipated that as a problem to be surmounted.'

'No,' Darcy said waspishly. 'I don't imagine you would have. Like I said—call someone else to provide you with any extra-curricular services you might require. I'm sure you can be discreet.' She looked at him, wondering just why this conversation was making her so angry. 'I would just avoid a three-in-a-bed romp—that won't endear you to Montgomery if it gets out like the last one did.'

Max made an irritated sound. 'For what it's worth that was a PR stunt for charity that ended up being leaked before we could explain it, so it never got used. You can't seriously think I'd be so crass?'

Darcy looked at him and cursed him. He looked positively angelic. Wrapped up in a demon. And of *course* he wouldn't be so crass. Max oozed sophistication. She should have known better. And now she'd revealed that she'd been keeping an eye on his exploits. *Damn him.*

She looked away. 'Whatever, Max—just don't make me look like a fool.'

'The same goes for you, you know,' came the softly delivered response.

Darcy looked at him and for a moment all she could see was the way Max had looked at her the other night, when she'd pulled back from his embrace, cheeks flushed, eyes glittering dangerously. 'Don't worry,' she said, as frigidly as she could, 'I won't have a problem curbing *my* urges.'

Max had muttered something she couldn't catch—something like *We'll see about that*—just as the car had pulled up outside the small plane.

Darcy's attention came back to the plane. Max was staring out of his window. Not goading her or looking at her with those mesmerising eyes. She remembered what he'd told her last night and how she'd wanted to leave his apartment—get away before he might see something on her face or in her expression. Empathy. A treacherous desire to help him achieve what he wanted.

'I didn't know your brother was a twin.'

Max turned his head slowly and looked at her. 'It's not really common knowledge.'

'I saw pictures of him…the wedding. You're not identical?'

Max shook his head and smiled, but it was hard. 'I'm prettier than my brother.' His self-mocking expression was anything *but* pretty. It was utterly masculine, making a mockery of 'pretty'.

Especially with that scar running from his temple to his jaw.

Darcy felt breathless. 'You said you're closer now?'

Max raised a brow. 'Did I?'

'Last night...you said you were working with him.'

Max's mouth tightened. 'For a cause—not because we sit up at night drinking cocoa and reminiscing about our childhood experiences.'

Darcy rolled her eyes at his sarcastic response just as the plane banked. She took the opportunity to escape Max's gaze and looked out to see Paris laid out in all its glory, the distinctive Eiffel Tower glinting in the distance. Fine. Obviously Max wasn't about to launch into any more confessionals. He'd probably already told her far more than he wanted to.

And she wasn't curious. Not at all.

Max watched as Darcy inspected the trays of rings laid out for their perusal. He almost smiled at her overwhelmed expression. She had been pretty slack-jawed since they'd walked into the opulent Rococo interior of one of the oldest jewellery establishments in the world. A byword in luxury, wealth and romance. These jewellers had supplied jewels for all the major royal houses, iconic movie stars and heads of state.

But he was still curbing the irritation he'd felt ever since Darcy's very stark insistence that they observe professional boundaries—marriage or no. Was the woman completely blind? All he had to do was come within two inches of her and the electricity was practically visible.

Even now he couldn't take his gaze off the way her breasts pressed lushly against the edge of the glass case they were sitting in front of. He'd noticed the sales assistant's eyes drop too, and had glared at the man so fiercely he'd almost dropped a tray of priceless rings.

Darcy's reminder that she would have been long gone if not for this wedding arrangement caused another ripple of irritation. Max wasn't used to things morphing out of his control. It was a sense of control hard won and fought for—literally.

But when Darcy looked at him with those huge blue eyes all he wanted to do was throw control out of the window and give in to pure basic instinct. And yet she had the wherewithal to sit there and draw a little prim circle around herself saying, *Not over the line.*

She looked at him now, and Max couldn't imagine a woman looking *less* enthusiastic to be here.

He frowned. 'What is it?'

She glanced at the assistant, who moved away for a moment, discreetly polishing a ring.

'I don't know what to choose—they're all so ridiculously expensive…I mean, you're going to insure the ring, right? I'd hate for anything to happen to it—especially when this isn't even for real.'

Max saw the clear turmoil on Darcy's face and it was like a punch to his gut to realise just how different she was from any other woman he might have brought to a place like this. They would have had absolutely no qualms about choosing the biggest and most sparkly bauble in the shop. And he would have indulged them without even thinking. It gave him a sense of distaste now.

He took her hand in his. It felt unbearably small and soft. 'Darcy, you're overthinking this. Just choose a ring. We'll get it insured. Okay?'

After a moment she nodded, and then said, 'Sorry, I'm probably making this boring for you.'

She looked back at the rings and some hair slipped over her shoulder, obscuring her face. Without thinking Max reached for it and tucked it behind her ear again. She looked at him and he couldn't resist. He leaned forward and pressed a kiss next to the corner of that surprisingly lush mouth.

Immediately her eyes went darker, but then they flashed. 'I told you—'

His hand gripped hers and he smiled as he said, 'We're buying a ring for our whirlwind engagement, *cara mia*, people are watching.'

She looked around quickly and then ducked her head, whispering fiercely, 'Fine…just in public.'

Max said nothing, but vowed right then to make sure they were in public as much as possible.

Darcy looked at the ring on her finger from different angles as Max discreetly paid the bill. Someone had delivered her a glass of champagne and she sipped it now. Grateful for the slightly numbing sensation. Numbing her from thinking about how choosing the ring had impacted on her so much.

It had brought up all sorts of unwelcome and tangled emotions. As a small girl she'd used to love going into her mother's jewellery box and looking at the glittering earrings and bracelets. But the engagement ring had been her favourite, made of nine baguette diamonds surrounded by sapphires and set in white gold.

Darcy had used to put it on, holding it in place and imagining herself in it, marrying a handsome prince.

And then one day it had disappeared. Darcy had asked her mother where it was, only to be told curtly that she'd sold it. That had been the beginning of the end of the fairytales in Darcy's imagination, as her parents' marriage had fractured and split apart over an agonising year of arguments and bitter recrimination.

Today the ring Darcy had chosen in the end had been far too close to something she might choose for real, but she hadn't been able to resist—some rogue devil had urged her on. A rectangular-shaped diamond, surrounded by smaller baguette diamonds, set in platinum. It was positively discreet when compared with some of the other choices, but right now it felt like an unbearably heavy weight on her hand.

'Ready?'

Darcy looked up to see Max waiting. She grew warm, thinking of him watching her as she'd been inspecting the ring, and almost sprang out of the chair.

'Ready.'

Max guided her solicitously out of the shop and Darcy couldn't help noticing a young couple as they passed, obviously head over heels in love. The pretty woman was crying as her boyfriend presented her with a ring.

Darcy caught Max's look and raised brows and scowled as he tutted, 'Now, *that's* not going to convince anyone.'

Just inside the clear revolving doors Max stopped her and turned her towards him. 'What—?' was all she managed to get out before Max cupped her jaw in one big hand and angled her face up to his so that he could kiss her.

Immediately the hot insanity of the other night slammed back into Darcy with such force that she had to cling onto his shirt to stay standing. It was an explicit kiss, and Darcy was dimly aware that someone like Max probably couldn't deliver a chaste kiss if his life depended on it. He was like a marauding pirate, sweeping in and taking no prisoners. It was hot, decadent, and the slide of Max's tongue against hers made her want to press her breasts against his chest and ease their ache.

When he pulled back she went with him, as if loath to break the contact. She opened her eyes and Max said smugly, 'That's a bit better.'

Darcy's brain felt sluggish as Max pulled her out of the shop, but it snapped back to crystal clarity when they faced a veritable wall of flashing lights.

'Max! Over here! Max! Who is the lucky lady? What's her name?'

The barrage of questions was deafening and terrifying. Max had his arm around Darcy and her hand was still gripping his shirt. She could feel the tension in his body as he said, in a masterful voice that sliced through the cacaphony, 'We will be releasing a statement on Monday. Until then please afford my fiancée and I some privacy.'

'Show us the ring!'

But Max's car materialised then, as if out of nowhere, and he was guiding Darcy into the back of it, shutting the baying mob outside as it took off smoothly into the Paris traffic.

Darcy vaguely heard Max curse, and then a glass was being pushed into her hands. She looked down, feeling a little blank and blinded.

'Take a sip, Darcy, you're in shock… *Maledizione*, I should have realised… You've never been papped before.'

When she didn't move he cursed again and lifted the glass to her lips, forcing liquid to trickle into her mouth and down her throat. She coughed as it smarted and burned and realised she was shaking from the adrenalin and shock of being in front of the paparazzi for the first time.

She looked at Max, who took the glass away and put it back in the car's mini-bar. 'How did they know?'

He had the grace to look slightly sheepish. 'I got my PR people to tip them off.'

Darcy thought of their kiss just inside the door, and all the lenses that must have been trained on them every moment, capturing her reaction. Not for one second did she want Max to know how angry it made her or how betrayed she felt. Stupid to think that a private moment had been invaded. It hadn't been a private moment—it had been manufactured.

'Well,' she said, as coolly as she could, 'I hope Montgomery sees it—or they'll have wasted an afternoon when they could have been chasing someone far more exciting.'

'I'm sorry. I should have warned you.'

Darcy feigned unconcern. 'Don't worry about it—at least it'll look authentic.'

'Good,' Max said briskly. 'Because we're going to a function in Rome this evening. It'll be our first official outing as a couple.'

Darcy looked at him and hated the way her voice squeaked as she said, 'Tonight?'

Max nodded. 'It's a charity gala.' His eyes flicked down over her chainstore dress and he glanced at his watch as he said, 'When we get back to Rome you'll be taken straight to meet with a stylist. She's going to put together a wardrobe for you. And a wedding dress.'

Darcy's hands curled into fists. She was barely aware that they were already on the outskirts of

Paris again, heading back to the airport. 'I might have plans for tonight.'

Max looked at her, and there was something distinctly proprietorial in his gaze. 'Any plans you have from now on are *my* plans. And I've been thinking: it'll look better if you move in with me. You should pack a weekend bag for now—we can move the rest of your stuff next week...'

Darcy didn't even bother opening her mouth, knowing resistance was futile. That was it. In the space of twenty-four hours her life had been neatly pulled inside out, and the worst thing was she'd agreed to it all.

CHAPTER FIVE

MAX LOOKED AT his watch again. *Where was she?* He'd meant to go and meet her at the apartment, but he'd been delayed in the office by a conference call to New York, so he'd changed there.

He'd texted Darcy to explain and got back a terse, Fine. See you there.

Max almost smiled; he couldn't imagine many women he knew texting him back like that. His almost-smile faded, though, when he thought of that morning and choosing the ring in Paris, and afterwards when they'd run into that wall of paparazzi.

He could still recall Darcy's jerk of fright and the way she'd burrowed into him instinctively. He'd felt like a heel. He'd totally underestimated how frightening that might be for someone who hadn't experienced it before. He was used to women revelling in the attention, preening, lingering… Darcy had been pale and shaking in the aftermath—not that she'd let it show for too long.

Something in Max's chest tightened. And then she was there, in the doorway of the function room, looking for him. Hair pulled up. One shoulder bare in an assymetrical dress that clung to her breasts, torso, and hips, before falling to the ground in a swirl of black silk and chiffon.

The room fell away, and the ever-present thrum of awareness made his blood sizzle.

How had he ever thought she was unassuming? She was stunning.

He could see her engagement ring from here, the brilliant flash of ice-white, and he pushed down the tightness in his chest. That same sense of protectiveness and possessiveness he'd felt earlier outside the jewellers hit him again, and he pushed that down too. It was nothing. It was the thrill of anticipated triumph over the deal that would finally take him away from that moment on the streets in Rome, when his own peers had seen him shabby and feral. Reduced to nothing.

Her eyes met his and he went forward to meet her.

* * *

Darcy saw Max almost as soon as she stopped in the doorway. Of course she did. He stood head and shoulders above most of the crowd. He was wearing a classic black tuxedo and she felt as if someone had hit her right between the eyes.

He'd made some effort to tidy his hair and it was swept back from his face now, dark blond and luxurious, but still with that trademark unruly length. And she could see from here that his jaw was clean-shaven.

In truth, she'd been glad of a little space from Max for the rest of the day—especially now she knew she'd be heading back to his apartment with him that night. She wasn't ready for that at all.

He was cutting a swathe through the crowd, heading straight for her, and—damn it—her breath was short again.

When he got to her he just looked at her for a long moment before slipping a hand across her bare shoulder and around the back of her neck. Her skin sizzled as his head came closer and his mouth—that perfect sensual mouth that rarely smiled—closed over hers.

She wanted to protest—*Stop kissing me!*—even as she knew he was only doing it for the benefit of their audience. But the fact was that every time he kissed her another little piece of her defences around him fell away.

There was nothing but blinding white heat for a second, as the firm contours of Max's mouth moved enticingly over hers, and then a rush of heat swelled all the way up her body from the pulse between her legs.

When he took his mouth away and pulled back she was dizzy, hot. It had been mere seconds. A chaste kiss on the mouth.

Max still had a hand around her neck. He was so close she could smell him, feel his heat around her. It was as if he was cocooning her slightly from the crowd and Darcy was reminded of the shock and vulnerability she'd felt in front of those paparazzi.

She pulled away from him.

'You look…beautiful.'

'You don't have to say that.'

Darcy felt exceedingly self-conscious in the dress the stylist had picked out for her to wear tonight. She glanced up at him from her eyeline, which was roughly around the centre of his chest—she'd been avoiding his gaze till now and his jaw was tight.

'It's not a line, Darcy, I mean it. You look… stunning.'

'I…' She couldn't speak. No man had ever complimented her like this before. She'd never felt *beautiful* before. But for a second, now, she did.

Max took her hand and led her into the throng, stopping to take the glass of champagne offered by a waiter before handing it to Darcy. She took a gulp, glad of the sustenance, aware of the interested looks they were getting—or rather that *she* was getting.

She hated the prickling feeling of being under scrutiny. The crowd in the ballroom of the exclusive Rome hotel was seriously intimidating. This was A-list territory. Actually, this made the A-list look like the B-list. She'd just spotted a European royal and an ex-American president talking together in a corner.

In a bid not to appear nervous, Darcy asked, 'So, what charity is benefiting from this function?'

Max glanced down at her. 'Numerous charities—I've nominated one I run with my brother.'

Darcy looked at Max, wondering again about his relationship with his brother, but she found herself distracted by his clean-shaven jaw and the white line of his scar that gave her a small jolt every time she saw it.

Just then a gong sounded and the crowd started to move into another room.

Max explained, with a cynical tinge to his voice, 'They'll get the charity auction and the posturing out of the way now, so that they can get on with the *really* important stuff.'

Max let go of her hand so she could sit down, and Darcy smiled politely at the man next to her. When Max took the seat next to hers she said, 'You mean the wheeling and dealing? The real reason why people are here?'

He looked at her approvingly. 'I'll make a proper cynic of you yet.'

Darcy felt a little hollow. She didn't need Max to make her a cynic. Her parents' spectacular break-up had gone a long way to that end already. Not to mention this pseudo-engagement.

She thought of something then, and looked at Max. 'You said to Montgomery that we'd be getting married in two weeks?'

He looked at her. 'We will. I've arranged for a special licence.'

Darcy felt as if she was drowning a little. 'Is it really necessary to go that far?'

Max nodded. 'It's just a piece of paper, Darcy. Neither of us really believes in marriage, do we?'

For a moment Darcy wasn't sure *what* she believed. She'd always sworn she'd avoid such a commitment, but she knew deep inside that some small part of her still harboured a wish that it could be different. Buying the ring today had tapped into it. And she hated it that this weakness was becoming evident here, in front of Max, under that gold gaze.

She forced a brittle smile. 'No, of course not. With our histories we'd be mad to expect anything more.' And she needed to remember that—especially when Max's touch and kisses scrambled her brain.

To take her mind off that she looked around and took in the extreme opulence. Even though her parents had always been well off—apart from her father's recessionary blip—she'd never moved in circles like this. Except for her time at Boissy. She grimaced at that memory, wondering if any of her old Boissy classmates were here. It was quite likely. This was definitely their stomping ground. Some of the offspring of Europe's most prominent royal families had been at the school.

The auction started and it was mesmerising. The sheer amounts being bid escalated well into the millions.

After one bid she gasped. 'Did someone *really* just buy an island?' Max's mouth quirked and Darcy immediately felt gauche. 'Don't laugh at me. I haven't been to anything like this before.'

There was a lull after the last few bids and he reached for her hand and lifted it up, turning it so that he could press a kiss to her palm. Darcy's heart-rate accelerated and she tried to pull her hand back, but he wouldn't let go, those eyes unnervingly direct on hers.

Feeling more and more discomfited, she whispered tetchily, 'We need to set some rules for an acceptable amount of PDAs. I wouldn't have thought you were a fan.'

Inwardly, Max reacted to that. Normally he wasn't. *At all*. He hated it when lovers tried to stake some kind of a public claim on him. But every time he touched Darcy he felt her resistance even as she melted against him. It was a potent mix of push and pull, and right now he wanted to touch her.

'You're big on rules and boundaries, aren't you?' He kept her hand in his when she would have pulled away, fascinated by the way colour washed in and out of her face so easily.

Her mouth tightened. 'They're necessary—especially when one is trying to be professional.'

Max chuckled, surprised to find himself enjoying being here with her so much. It had been a long time since he'd seen anyone interested in a charity auction. 'I don't think I need to tell you our professional boundaries are well and truly breached.'

She hissed at him. 'As if I'm not aware of that. Do I need to remind *you* that if it wasn't for this crazy marriage farce I'd be long gone by now?'

Something inside Max went cold. She would be gone because of what had happened in his office that night. He didn't doubt it. But Max knew now that he would have felt compelled to try and persuade her to stay...or to seduce her properly. She'd set a fire alight that night, and a very unwelcome and insidious suspicion occurred to him. Had he on some level wanted to keep her at all costs? Precipitating his flashbulb idea of marrying her?

Panic washed through him and he handed her hand back. 'You're right. We don't want to overdo it—no one would believe it.'

The sudden hurt that lanced Darcy made her suck in a breath. Of course they wouldn't believe it. Because why on earth would someone like Max—a golden god—be with someone like *her*?

She got up jerkily and Max frowned.

'Darcy—wait. I didn't mean it like—'

But she cut him off with a tight smile and muttered something about the bathroom, making her escape.

Everyone was standing up now and moving, starting to go back out to the main ballroom, where a world-famous band were about to play a medley of their greatest hits. She found a blissfully empty bathroom off the main foyer and looked at herself in the mirror with horror.

In spite of Max's cruel words she was flushed, and her eyes looked wide and bright enough to be feverish. Just because he'd held her hand? *Pathetic.*

She ran the cold water and played it over her wrists, as if that could douse the fire in her blood. *Damn Max anyway.* He shouldn't have the power to hurt her.

Sounds came from outside—voices. She quickly dried her hands and left just as some women were coming in on a wave of expensive perfume. They were all chattering, and stopped abruptly as soon as they saw her.

Darcy pinned a smile on her face and tried not to let the fact that they'd obviously been discussing *her* intimidate her.

As she approached the ballroom again Darcy saw Max standing at the main door, hands in his pockets. He looked…magnificent. *Hateful.* Proud. But also apart. Like a lone wolf. *Good.* A man like him didn't deserve friends. And that just made Darcy feel horrible.

He turned around and saw her and she could almost feel the place where the cold water had run on her wrists sizzle.

He frowned as she came closer. 'Are you okay?'

Now she felt silly for rushing off. 'Fine. Needed to go to the bathroom.' She thought a little despondently that his usual lovers probably didn't suffer the mundane bodily functions of mortals—and certainly never mentioned them to him.

He took her arm. 'We're done now. Let's go.'

Suddenly the thought of going back to his apartment with him loomed like a spectre in the dark. Anger at him pierced her, and anger at herself—for letting him hurt her so easily.

A rogue voice made her dig her heels in and say, 'Actually, I'm not ready to go yet.'

He looked at her, not a little stunned. He was not used to people saying no to him.

She tipped up her chin and took a moment of inspiration from the music nearby. 'I like this band. I want to dance.'

Now Max looked horrified. 'Dance?' Clearly he never indulged in such pedestrian activities.

She arched a brow, enjoying needling Max a little. 'Dance, Max. You know—a recreational social activity designed to bring people together in a mutually satisfactory way.'

Clearly angry now, Max moved closer to Darcy and pulled her into his body. 'I can do a "mutually satisfactory" activity, *dolcezza*, if that's what you're looking for—but it's not called dancing.'

Darcy's breath hitched. She should have known better than to tease him. She was serious. 'A dance, Max. That's what I'm talking about.'

He lifted a hand and cupped her jaw, for all the world the besotted fiancé. She cursed. She was playing right into his hands.

'Fine, then. Let's dance.'

Max took her hand in a firm and slightly too tight grip that told her of his irritation and led her onto the dance floor just in time for a slow number. Darcy cursed herself again for opening her big mouth.

He turned and gathered her close and she had to put her arms around his neck. He looked down at her and said mockingly, 'Forgive me. I had no idea you were so eager to make our charade look even more authentic.'

Darcy snorted, and then went still when one of Max's hands moved lower, to just above her buttocks, pressing her even closer. She closed her eyes in frustration for a moment—as if she needed to be reminded that he resented this PDA as much as she did.

And then she felt his hand brush some hair back off her cheek and he said, in a different tone of voice that set off flutters in her belly, 'Darcy, look at me.'

Reluctantly she opened her eyes, far too aware of his lean, hard body pressed against hers.

'I think you misunderstood me before…I meant no one would believe it because I don't usually indulge in any kind of overt affection with lovers in public.'

Darcy hated it that he'd seen her hurt. She shrugged. 'It's cool, Max, you don't have to explain anything.'

Even so, the hurt dissipated like a traitorous little fog.

'The problem is,' he went on, as if she hadn't spoken, 'I can't seem to stop myself from touching you.'

She looked up at him, and they stopped moving on the dance floor while everyone kept going around them. Max pressed against the small of her back, moving her closer to his body, where she could feel the distinctive thrust of his arousal.

Now he looked intense. 'This is not usual for me, Darcy.'

She was barely aware of where they were any

more, and she whispered, 'You think it's usual for me?'

Max started to move again subtly, ratcheting up the tension between them. Panic flared at the thought of going back to his apartment. 'Max, this isn't... We can't do this. We need to keep this pro-professional.'

Great. She was stuttering now. All she knew was that if Max seduced her she wouldn't have anything left to hold him at bay with. He'd already swept through her life like a wrecking ball.

He arched a wicked brow. 'You know what I think of professionalism? It's overrated.'

And then he kissed her, deeply and explicitly, and Darcy knew she was right to fear him—*this*. Because she could feel her very cells dissolving, merging into his. She was losing herself.

She pulled back with effort. '*No*, Max.'

A faster, more upbeat song was playing now, and she and Max were motionless in the middle of the floor. He grabbed her hand and pulled her from the throng. Her legs were like jelly.

Once away from the dance floor Max stopped and turned to Darcy, running a hand through his hair, an intense look on his face.

'Look, Darcy—' He stopped suddenly as something caught his eye over Darcy's head. He cursed volubly and an infinitely hard expression came over his face.

Darcy frowned and looked behind her to see a stunningly beautiful woman in the far corner of the room. Something pulled at a vague memory. She was wearing a skin-tight black dress that shimmered and clung to her spectacular figure. Dark hair was swept back and up from her high-cheekboned face, and jewels sparkled at her ears and throat.

Darcy's insides cramped a little as she wondered if it was an ex-lover of Max's she'd seen in a magazine.

He was propelling them across the room before she could say anything, and as they got closer she could see that the woman was older than she'd imagined—but incredibly well-preserved.

She was arguing with a tall, handsome man, holding a glass of champagne and gesticulating. The wine was slopping messily onto the ground.

The man looked at Max with visible relief and more than a little irritation. He said curtly, 'I've had enough—you're welcome to her, Roselli.'

The woman whirled around, and just as Darcy noticed with a jolt of shock that she had exactly the same colour eyes as Max he was saying, in a tone tinged with steel, 'Mamma.'

His mother issued a stream of vitriol. Her eyes were unfocused and there was a sheen of perspiration on her face. Her pupils were tiny pinpricks. It was shocking to come face-to-face with Max's mother like this, and it made Darcy's heart clench to think he'd probably only told her half of what she'd been like.

The other man had walked away. Max's mother made as if to go after him but Max let go of Darcy's arm to stop her, taking her glass away and handing it to Darcy. His mother screeched and Darcy could see people looking.

Max had his mother in a firm grip now, and he said to Darcy, 'I'll take her home. If you wait here I'll get my driver to come back for you.'

Darcy was about to agree, but then she said quickly, 'Shouldn't I go with you? It'll look a little odd if I don't.'

Max was clearly reluctant to have Darcy witness this scene—she had a keen sense that he wouldn't allow many, if *any* people to witness it—but he obviously realised she was right.

'Fine, let's go.'

Staff had ordered Max's car to come round and he got into the back with his mother, who was remonstrating volubly with Max now. Darcy got in the front, her nerves jumping. Max was apparently used to this, and was on his phone making a terse call.

When they pulled up outside an exclusive apartment block in a residential part of Rome a man in a suit was waiting. Max introduced him as Dr. Marconi and he came in with them. Once inside a palatial apartment Max and the doctor and his mother disappeared into one of the rooms, with the door firmly closed behind them.

Darcy waited in the foyer, feeling extremely out of place. Max's mother was shouting now, and crying. Darcy could hear Max's voice, low and firm.

The shouting stopped.

After a long while Max re-emerged and Darcy stood up from where she'd been sitting on a gilt-edged chair.

'How is she?'

Max's hair was dishevelled, as if he'd been running his hands through it, and his bow tie was undone. He looked grim. 'I'm sorry you had to witness that. I would have introduced you, but as you could probably tell her response was unlikely to be coherent.'

'You've dealt with this before...?'

Max smiled, but it didn't reach his eyes. 'You could say that. She's a drug addict. And an alcoholic. The man at the party was her latest enabler, but evidently he's had enough. So what'll happen now is she'll enter an exclusive rehab centre, that's got more in common with a five-star resort than a medical facility, and in about a month, when she's detoxed, she'll rise like a phoenix from the ashes and start all over again.'

The other man emerged now, and spoke in low tones to Max before taking his leave after bidding goodnight to Darcy. Max turned to her.

'You should go. My driver is outside. I'm going to wait for a nurse to come and then make sure my mother is settled before I go. I'll see you in the morning.'

Clearly he wanted her to go now. She backed away to the door.

'Goodnight, Max.' She turned back from the door to say impulsively, 'I'm sorry...about your mother. If there's anything I can do...' She trailed off, feeling helpless.

'Thank you,' Max said shortly. 'But it's not your problem. I'll deal with it.'

For a fleeting moment Darcy thought that if this was a real engagement then it would be her problem too. She wondered if a man like Max would ever lean on anyone but himself and felt an almost overwhelming urge to go to him and offer...what?

She left quickly, lest Max see anything of her emotions on her face.

In the car on the way home Darcy had a much keener and bleaker sense of what things must have been like for Max when he'd left Brazil with his mother. The fact that he'd ended up on the streets wasn't so hard to believe now, and the empathy she felt for him was like a heavy weight in her chest.

A few hours later Max sat back in the chair in his dark living room and relished the burn of the whisky as it slid down his throat. He finally felt the tension in his body easing. He'd left his mother sleeping, with a nurse watching over her.

When he'd seen Elisabetta Roselli across the function room earlier tension had gripped him, just as it always did. It was a reflex born of years of her inconsistant mothering. Never knowing what to expect. And even though he was an adult now, and she couldn't affect his life that way any more, his first reaction had been one of intense fear and anxiety. And he hated it.

Darcy... He could still see her face in his mind's eye when she'd turned back from the door, concerned. The fact that she'd handled seeing his mother in that state impacted on him in some deep place he had no wish to explore.

His brother had not had to suffer dealing with the full vagaries of their mother. Max was used to dealing with it on his own... But for a moment, with Darcy looking back at him, he'd actually wanted to reach out and pull her to him, feel her close, wrapping her arms around him...

A soft noise made Max's head jerk up. Darcy stood silhouetted in the doorway of the living room as if conjured right out of his imagination. She was wearing loose sleep pants and a singlet vest that did little to hide those lush heavy breasts, the tiny waist. Her hair was long and tumbled about her shoulders.

'Sorry, I heard a noise…you're back. Is she… your mother…is she okay?'

Max barely heard Darcy. He was so consumed with the sight of her breasts, recalling with a rush of blood to his groin how they'd felt pressed against him on that dance floor.

Damn it to hell. He didn't want to want her. Especially not when he felt so raw after the incident with his mother. But even from across the room her huge blue eyes seemed to see right through him—into him. Right down to the darkest part of him.

It made something twist inside him. A need to push her away, push her back. Avoid her scrutiny.

'Getting into character as my wife already, Darcy? Careful, now—I might believe you're starting to like me. I guess having an addict for a mother is bound to score *some* sympathy points…'

CHAPTER SIX

DARCY IMMEDIATELY PALED in the dim lighting, and Max didn't even have time to regret the words that had come out of his mouth before her eyes were flashing blue sparks.

'I know you're a ruthless bastard, Max, but I've never thought you were unnecessarily cruel. If that's the way this will play out then you can find yourself another convenient wife.'

She whirled around and was almost gone before Max acknowledged the bitter tang of instant remorse and shot up out of his chair, closed the distance between them and grabbed her arm in his hand, stopping her in her tracks.

He cursed and addressed the back of that glossy head. 'Darcy. I'm sorry.'

After a long moment she turned round. She was so tiny in her bare feet, and it reminded him of how she'd fitted against him earlier that day, making him aware of an alien need to protect, to cosset.

Her eyes were huge, wounded. He cursed himself silently. 'I'm sorry,' he said again, aware that he'd probably never uttered those words to anyone.

'You should be.'

Her voice was husky and it had an effect on every nerve-ending in Max's body.

'You didn't deserve that.'

'No, I didn't.'

And then, because it felt like the most natural thing in the world, as well as the most urgent, Max took her other arm and pulled her round to face him. The air crackled between them. He could see Darcy's breasts rise and fall faster with her breathing, and he was so hard he ached.

He dipped his head and pressed his mouth to Darcy's, drawing her up against him. She was as still as a statue for a long moment, as if determined to resist, and then on a small indrawn breath her mouth opened under Max's and the blood roared in his head.

His hands dropped and settled on her waist, over the flimsy fabric of her vest, relishing the contours of her tiny waist. She triggered something very primal in him in a way no other woman ever had.

His tongue stroked into her mouth, finding hers and tangling with it hotly. His erection jerked in his pants in response and he groaned softly.

Darcy tasted like the sweetest nectar on earth, but her small sharp tongue was a pointed reminder that she had an edge. That only fired up his blood even more. She was soft, sweet, malleable...and melting into him like his hottest fantasy.

Max took ruthless advantage, deepening the kiss, his hands gripping her waist, pulling her into him, feeling his aching hardness meet the soft resistance of her body. Her breasts were full, pressing against him, and his hand snaked under her vest, spreading out over her lower back. Her skin was silky and hot to the touch.

Lust such as he'd never experienced had him in a grip so strong he couldn't think beyond obeying this carnal need.

Darcy was dimly aware of a very distant voice in her head, screaming at her to stop and pull back. Moments ago she'd been blisteringly angry with

Max. And hurt. But she didn't care any more. She was in his arms and her world was made up of heat and glorious pounding desire.

Every part of her exulted in his masculinity and his sheer size. Big hands were smoothing up her back, lifting her vest until it snagged under her breasts. He pulled away from her mouth and Darcy sucked in much needed oxygen—but it didn't go to her brain, it seemed only to fuel the hunger in her body.

Max's mouth feathered kisses along her jawbone and down to the sensitive part of her neck just under her ear.

The scent of sex was musky in the air and it was mixed with something very feminine. *Her desire.* Oh, God. She was so weak, but she didn't care any more.

When he pulled back to take her hand in his and lead her over to the sofa she went with him without hesitation. He sat down and guided her over him so that she ended up with her knees either side of his thighs, straddling his lap, his erection a hard ridge between her legs.

Some vital part of her brain had abdicated all responsibility for this situation. It felt dangerously liberating. He was looking at her with such dark intent that she felt dizzy even as her hands were already on his shirt, fumbling with the buttons, eager to explore the wide expanse of his chest.

He said thickly, '*Dio*, I want you so much.'

Darcy couldn't speak. So she bent her head and kissed him again. His hands gripped her waist for a moment before exploring upwards, pulling her vest up and over her breasts, baring them.

He broke the kiss and looked at her, eyes wide, feverish. *'Si bella...'*

He cupped one breast in his hand and squeezed the firm flesh. Darcy bit her lip at the exquisite sensation, and then cried out when he leaned forward and took the straining tip into his mouth, sucking it deep before letting it pop out and then ministering to her other breast with the same attention.

She wasn't even aware that her hips were making subtle circular motions on Max's lap, seeking to assuage the building tension at her core, where the slide of his erection between her legs was a wicked temptation. She only became aware when his hand moved down to her buttocks and held her there. His arousal was thrusting between them, touching her intimately through their clothes. She was pulsating, all over.

A wave of incredible tenderness moved over her as she saw his scar, gleaming white in the low lights. Without thinking Darcy reached out and traced it gently, running her finger down the raised and jagged length. Then she bent to kiss it.

And just as she did so the wave of tenderness finally triggered some faulty self-protection mechanism and she tensed all over, her mouth hovering just over Max's scar.

What the hell was she doing?

He'd just been a complete bastard and yet after a brief apology and a kiss hotter than Hades she was writhing in his lap, about to let emotion overwhelm her! A man who saw her as just a means to an end.

What was even worse was that she'd already seen some pictures online, of them in Paris, outside the jewellers. She looked like a rabbit caught in the headlights, small and chubby next to Max's tall, lean form, clutching at him. It was galling. Mortifying how ill-matched they were.

Darcy scrambled up and off Max's lap so fast

she nearly fell backwards. She tugged her vest down over straining breasts.

Max sat forward, his shirt half open, deliciously dishevelled. 'Darcy…what the *hell*?'

Darcy's voice was shaky. 'This is a mistake.'

Every masculine bone in Max's body was crying out for completion, satisfaction. He could barely see straight. He'd been moments away from easing his erection free of confinement, ripping Darcy's clothes off and embedding himself so deeply inside her he'd see stars.

He hated it that she seemed to have more control than him—that she'd been the one to pull back. The rawness he'd felt earlier had returned. He felt exposed.

He stood up in a less than graceful movement, his body still clamouring for release, but he was damned if he was going to admit that to Darcy.

He bit out, 'I don't play games, Darcy, and I don't believe in mistakes. I believe in choices. And you need to be honest with yourself and make one.'

Darcy looked up at him for a long moment and the very thin edges of Max's control threatened to fray completely. But then she took a step back and said in a low voice, 'You're right. I'm sorry. It won't happen again.'

Frustration clawed at Max with talons of steel. That was *not* the answer he'd wanted to hear. As she moved to walk away he reached out and took her arm again, not liking the way she tensed.

'Damn it, Darcy. We both want this.'

She turned her head and looked at him. 'No, Max, we don't.'

She pulled free and walked quickly from the room.

Two weeks later

'I do hope that you haven't put me anywhere near your father. Honestly, if he turns up with his latest bimbo—'

'*Mother.* Please stop.' Darcy tried to keep the exasperation out of her voice. 'You're not near my father, you're at opposite ends of the reception lunch table *and* the registry office.'

Her mother, as petite as Darcy but über-slim sniffed. 'Well, that's good.'

Darcy sighed. She and Max had agreed that it would look better to have family there, and that they could serve as witnesses. Her parents were as bad as each other in different ways: her passionate Italian mother was on a constant quest to find security with ever younger and richer men, and her hopelessly romantic father got his heart broken on a regular basis by a stream of never-ending gold-diggers who saw Tom Lennox coming from a mile away.

She forced a smile at her mother in the mirror, not wanting to invite questions about anything beyond the superficial.

To say that the last two weeks had been a strain was an understatement. Luckily work had kept Darcy busy, preparing for the final reckoning with Montgomery. But the personal tension between Max and her had almost reached breaking point. Even though they'd barely seen each other in his apartment. He worked late most nights, so she was in bed when he returned, and he was gone before her in the morning. And Darcy, of course, had refrained from any more dangerous nocturnal wanderings.

Even now she burned with humiliation when she thought of the concern she'd felt when she'd seen him that night, staring broodingly into his drink. Alone... Vulnerable... *Ha!* The man was about as vulnerable as reinforced steel.

Darcy was sure that he'd only been in London to meet with Montgomery for the last two days to get away from her, and she hated how that stung.

Since that night in his apartment he'd been cool to the point of icy. And she only had herself to blame. She'd been the weak one. Blowing hot and then cold. Running away because she couldn't handle the thought of Max breaching the final intimacy, afraid of what would happen to her if he did.

No doubt he was used to women who knew what they wanted and went after it—and him. No qualms. No questions. Maybe he'd been seeing one of those women in London, discreetly?

Her mother tugged at the back of her dress now, tutting. 'Honestly, Darcy, why couldn't you have bought a nice *long* dress? This one's more suitable for a cocktail party. This *is* quite likely to be your only wedding day, you know.'

Darcy welcomed the distraction and said fervently, 'I'm counting on it. And it's a registry office wedding, Mother. This dress is perfectly suitable.'

Her mother sniffed and tweaked Darcy's chignon, where a mother of pearl comb held the short veil back from her face. 'Well, I suppose it *is* a nice dress, for all that,' she admitted grudgingly.

Darcy ran a critical eye over herself, feeling slightly disembodied at the thought that she was getting married that day. To Max Fonseca Roselli. The dress was off-white satin, coming to just over her knee. It was a simple sheath design, overlaid with exquisitely delicate lace. It covered her arms and up to her throat.

It's fine, she told herself, hating that the little girl in her still yearned for something long and swirling…romantic.

Wanting to avoid any further scrutiny, she said to her mother, '*You* look gorgeous.'

Her mother preened—predictably. She was indeed stunning, in a dusky pink dress and matching jacket. An exotic fascinator was arranged in her luxurious dark hair, which was piled high.

As she zipped up her dress at the back Darcy referred to her mother's comment about her father. 'It's not as if you haven't brought your own arsenal, Mother.'

Viola Bianci glared at her daughter. 'Javier and I are very much in love.'

Darcy just arched a brow. From what she'd seen of the permatanned Spanish Lothario, he was very much in love with *himself*, but he was obviously enjoying parading the very well preserved and beautiful older woman on his arm. For whatever reason—whether it was love or something less—he was lavishing attention and money on her mother, so Darcy desisted from making any more comments.

Her mother came in front of her now, to pull the veil over her face, but she stopped and looked at Darcy.

'*Carina*…are you sure you're doing the right thing?' Her mother looked slightly discomfited for a moment. 'I mean, after your father and I… Well, our break-up…I always got the impression that you weren't really into marrying *anyone*.'

A familiar impulse to deflect any concern about her rose up, and even though Darcy recognised that it was totally misplaced she put a hand on her mother's arm and said reassuringly, 'Don't worry. I know what I'm doing.'

And she did, she told herself.

Her mother wasn't finished, though. 'But are you in love with him, Darcy? You might think I don't notice much, but one thing I've always known about you is that you'd never settle for anything less than a lifetime commitment—whether it's through marriage or not.'

Darcy all but gaped at her mother. Since when did Viola Bianci display any perspicacity in looking into her daughter's psyche? It slammed into her gut and made her want to recoil and protect herself. *Lifetime commitment.* Was that really what she wanted? As a result of her experiences? More than a sense of security and a successful career?

Her mouth was opening and closing ineffectually. Finally she croaked, 'I… Well, I do…I mean, I am—'

Just then a knock came on the door and one of the wedding planner's team popped her head round the door. 'It's time to go.'

Saved by the bell—almost literally. As Darcy's mother began to flap, gathering up her personal belongings and Darcy's bouquet, she'd never been so glad for her gnat-like attention span. Clearly she wasn't that concerned about whether Darcy was marrying for true love or not—and frankly that one insight, no matter how erroneous Darcy assured herself it was, was discombobulating enough.

The registry office felt tiny and stifling to Max, but as he was about to ask for the window to be opened he saw that it was already open. He'd been talking to Darcy's father, who was a pleasant affable man, completely preoccupied with his much younger glamorous girlfriend, whom Max had categorised as a gold-digger in seconds. She was busy making eyes at Max whenever Tom Lennox's back was turned.

Max had to curb the urge to scowl at her. She was tall, slim, blonde and undeniably beautiful, but his head was still filled with the way Darcy had felt straddling his lap that night, the size of her tiny waist spanned by his hands. The feel of that hard nipple against his tongue. The scent of her.

Hell. It had been two weeks ago. He was usually hard-pressed to recall any liaison more than twenty-four hours after it had happened. Making love with women was a very pleasurable but transitory thing in his life.

He didn't wake up at night sweating, with the sheets tangled around his aching body like a vise. *He did now.* Which was why he'd been in London for the last two days, putting himself through more unsatisfactorily inconclusive meetings with Cecil Montgomery.

The man was still insisting that all would be revealed in a week's time. *Damn him.* The one thing easing his frustration was that Montgomery's attitude had definitely changed since Max had announced his marriage to Darcy. Gone was the slightly condescending and derisory tone. There was a new respect that Max couldn't deny.

So this would be worth it. The fact that Darcy was driving him slowly insane would all be worth it.

Max felt a prickling sensation across his skin and looked up just as the few people gathered in the room hushed.

She was here. And he couldn't breathe, seeing how beautiful she looked. It felt as if he hadn't seen her in weeks, not two paltry days.

She stood in the doorway with a woman he assumed to be her mother. But he only saw Darcy. The delicious curves of her body were outlined in a white lace dress. A short veil came to her chin, obscuring her face. But he could make out her huge blue eyes even through the gauzy material and he felt his belly tighten with something like…emotion?

She was doing this for him. A monumental favour. *You're paying her*, pointed out a pragmatic voice. But still… This went above and beyond payment.

It was gratitude he felt. Gratitude that she was doing this for him. That was all.

Her mother moved ahead of her, smiling winsomely at Max, who forced a smile back. But he couldn't take his eyes off Darcy as she came the short distance between the chairs towards him. She held a bouquet of flowers in front of her—not that Max could have said what they were.

And then she was beside him, and he was turning to the front, acutely aware of her body heat and her scent. He felt an urge to reassure her but pushed it down. Darcy knew what this was. She was doing it for her own reasons and because he was paying her handsomely.

He frowned minutely. Why had she asked for that specific amount of money?

'Signor Roselli?'

Max blinked. *Damn.* The registrar repeated the words for Max, which he duly recited, and then he was facing Darcy. He felt slightly dizzy. Rings were exchanged. Darcy's hands were tiny, her fingers cool as they slid the ring onto his finger. Her voice was low, clear. No hesitation.

And then he was lifting her veil back from her face and all he could see was an ocean of blue. And those soft lips, trembling ever so slightly.

'You may kiss your bride.'

He heard the smile in the registrar's voice but he was oblivious as he cupped Darcy's small face between his hands, tipping it up towards him, and bent to kiss her.

Darcy's mouth was still tingling and she had to stop herself from putting her fingers to it, to feel if it was swollen. Her hand was in Max's firm grip, her bouquet in the other hand, as he led her through the foyer of the exclusive Rome hotel and into the dining room where an intimate lunch was being held.

Along with her parents, who had been their witnesses, Max had invited his brother and new sister-in-law, and some business associates from Max's company.

Darcy felt like an absolute fraud, and was not looking forward to being under the inspection of people she didn't know well. Max made her feel so *raw*—and even more so now, after two weeks of minimal contact.

Max turned at the door to the dining room, where their guests were waiting, stopping her. His grip on her hand tightened and compelled her to look up at him. She'd been too wound up to really take him in before now, but his dark grey morning suit along with a silk cravat made him look even more handsome and masculine. He could have stepped out of the nineteenth century. A rake if ever there was one. Even though he was clean-shaven and his unruly hair was tamed. Well, as tamed as it would ever be.

Darcy felt a rogue urge to reach up and run her fingers through it, to muss it up.

'Okay?'

She looked deep into those golden eyes and felt her heart skip a beat. She nodded minutely.

Max cupped her face with his hand and rubbed a thumb across her lower lip. Her body clamoured, telling her how much she'd missed his touch.

And then he tensed. Darcy looked to the side to see a tall dark man with possibly the most beautiful woman she'd ever seen in her life. White-blonde hair and piercing ice-blue eyes. But they were warm, and the woman was smiling at Darcy.

Max took his hand away from her jaw and stood straight. She could feel the tension in his form. 'Darcy, I'd like you to meet Luca Fonseca, my brother, and his wife Serena.'

Max's twin was as tall, and as powerfully built as he was, but much darker, with black hair and dark blue eyes.

Darcy shook hands with both of them and Serena came closer to say, 'Your dress is beautiful.'

Darcy made a small face, feeling completely inadequate in the presence of this goddess. 'I felt less might be more, considering it was a registry office wedding.'

Serena made a sound of commiseration and said, 'My husband and I had a beach wedding, just us and close family, and I can't tell you how relieved I was not to be paraded down some aisle like a wind-up doll.'

Darcy let out a little laugh, surprised that she was so warm and friendly. She felt a pang to realise that she probably wouldn't ever meet her again after this.

A staff member interrupted them to let them know that everyone was ready for Max and Darcy to make their entrance as a married couple. Luca and Serena went inside and Darcy took a deep breath, glad that it was only a handful of guests. Max took her hand and she pasted a bright smile on her face as they walked into a welcome of clapping and cheers.

They were soon separated and caught up in a round of congratulations and chatter. Darcy felt even more like a fraud, aware of Max's tall form on the other side of the room as he spoke to his brother. She felt as if she had *'fake bride'* emblazoned on her forehead.

When there was a lull Serena surprised her by coming over and handing her a glass of champagne.

Darcy took a grateful sip. 'Thanks, I needed that.'

Serena frowned minutely. 'Are you okay? You look a little pale.'

Darcy smiled weakly. 'It's just been a bit of a whirlwind two weeks.'

Serena was about to say something when her husband Luca appeared at her side and wound his arm possessively around her waist. They shared a look so intimate that Darcy felt like a voyeur. And something worse: *envy.*

To Darcy's intense relief a gong sounded then, indicating that lunch would be served. She siezed on the excuse to break away and find her seat, and pushed down the gnawing sense of emptiness that had no place here, at a fake wedding.

The tension that gripped Max whenever he saw his brother had eased somewhat by the time they were sipping fragrant coffee after lunch. He looked around at the guests at the long table. He and Darcy were at the head and she was leaning towards the man on her left, one of Max's accountants.

This wedding was putting him in pole position to achieve everything he'd ever wanted: the ultimate respect among his peers. So why wasn't he feeling a sense of triumph? Why on earth was he preoccupied with his very fake wife and how delectable she looked in her wedding dress? How he'd like to peel it bit by bit from that luscious body?

At that moment he spied his brother and his wife, sitting halfway down the table. They were side by side and looking at one another with utter absorption. It made something dark twist inside him.

He shouldn't have invited them. All anyone would have to do would be to look at Luca and Serena and realise how flimsy the façade of his marriage to Darcy was.

Once again his brother was effortlessly proving Max's lack. And worse was the evidence that whatever blows Luca had been dealt in his life they hadn't touched some deep part of him, tainting him for ever. For the first time, Max felt more than envy—he felt hollow.

'What is it? You look as if you're about to murder someone.'

The low voice came close to his ear and Max turned his head to see Darcy's face, a small frown between her eyes. He felt exposed—and frustrated. There was a futile sense of rage in his gullet that was old and dark, harking back to that one cataclysmic day in his childhood. Still to be bound by that day was galling.

He acted instinctively—seeking something he couldn't put a name to. Perhaps an antidote to the darkness inside him. An escape from the demons nipping at his heels. He uncurled his hand and put it around Darcy's waist, tugging her into him before claiming her mouth in a kiss that burned like wildfire through his veins.

It didn't bring escape, though. It brought carnal hunger, and a need that only she seemed able to tap into. Incensed that she could do this to him so easily—and here, in front of witnesses—made Max deepen the embrace. He felt rather than heard Darcy's moan as both hands moved around her back.

Eventually some sliver of sanity seemed to pierce the heat haze in his brain and he pulled back. Darcy took a second to open her eyes. Her mouth was pink and swollen, her breasts moving rapidly against him.

And then he saw her come to her senses. Those blue eyes went from hot to cold in seconds and she tried to pull free, but Max didn't let her go, keeping her attention on him.

Darcy couldn't seem to suck enough oxygen into her heaving lungs. When she could, she hissed at Max, 'What the *hell* was that little cave-man move?'

She knew damn well that his urge to indulge in that very public display of affection hadn't been entirely inspired by the need to fool their guests, because the look on his face just before he'd kissed her had been dark and haunted. It struck a raw nerve.

She pushed herself free of Max's embrace and stood up.

He stood up too, frowning. 'Where are you going?'

Darcy whispered angrily, 'I'm taking ten minutes' break from this charade—if that's all right with you?'

She forced a poilte smile at their guests, who had now started moving around after lunch, but didn't stop, heading straight for a secluded balcony through an open set of French doors. She needed air. *Now.*

She went and stood at the stone wall and looked

out over Rome, basking benignly in the midafternoon sun. It was idyllic, and a million miles from the turmoil in her belly and her head.

Damn Max and his effortless ability to push her buttons. The galling thing was she didn't even know what button he was pushing. She just knew she was angry with him, and she hated feeling like a puppet on a string. This was a mistake. No amount of money was worth this. She'd happily live as a nomad for the rest of her life if she could just be as far away from Max as possible.

Liar.

'Darcy?'

She closed her eyes. No escape.

Darcy turned from the view. It was the thread of concern in his voice that made her glance at him, but his face was unreadable.

She looked at him accusingly. 'Why did you kiss me like that? It wasn't just to put on a show for people.'

'No,' he admitted reluctantly, 'it wasn't just for that.'

A pain that Darcy knew she shouldn't be feeling gripped her when she thought of the anger and frustration she'd sensed in the kiss.

'It's one thing to be wilfully and knowingly used for another's benefit, and to agree to that, but I won't let you take the fact that I'm not the lover you want out on me.'

Max's eyes widened. And then he came in front of her and put his hands on the wall either side of her, caging her in. In a low, fierce voice he said, 'That statement is so far from the truth it's not even funny. The only woman I am remotely interested in is right in front of me.'

Darcy swallowed and tried not to let Max's proximity render her stupid. 'But you were angry...I could feel it.'

Max pushed himself off the wall and ran a hand around his jaw. He stood beside Darcy and looked out at the view. Then he sighed and without looking at her said, 'You're right. I was angry.'

Darcy rested her hip against the wall, her own anger diffusing treacherously. 'Why?'

Max's mouth twitched, but it wasn't a smile. More a reflex. 'My brother, primarily. I saw them—him and his wife...'

Without elaborating Darcy knew exactly what he meant. She'd seen it too. Their almost unbearable intimacy.

Max shrugged and looked down for a moment. 'He gets to me like no one else can. Pushes my buttons. I always feel like I'm just catching up to him, two steps behind.'

Darcy could see it then: the intense hunger Max had to feel he wasn't in competition with his brother any more. Whatever had happened when their parents had split up had marked these two men indelibly.

Feeling tight inside, she said, 'Well, I don't like being used to score a point. Next time find some-one else.'

She went to move away, to go back inside, but Max caught her before she could leave with his hands around her waist, holding her fast. His eyes were blazing down into hers.

'I kissed you because I want you, Darcy. If there was anger there at my brother it was forgot-ten the moment my mouth touched yours. I do not want you to be under any illusions. When I kiss you I know exactly who I'm kissing and why.'

Darcy stared up at him, transfixed by the in-tensity of his expression.

'*Maledizione.* I can't think when you look at me like that.'

He pulled her closer and Darcy fell against him, unsteady in her shoes. She braced her hands against his chest. He was warm. Hard.

'Max…' Darcy protested weakly—*too* weakly. 'There's no one here to see.'

'Good,' he said silkily. 'Because this is not motivated by any reason other than the fact that I want you.'

One hand cupped the back of Darcy's head and the other was tight around her waist, almost lifting her off her feet. When Max's mouth met hers she was aghast to realise how badly she wanted it, and she met him with a fervour that should have embarrassed her. But it didn't. She wound her arms around his neck, her breasts swelling against his chest.

He backed Darcy into the wall, so it supported her, and their kiss was bruising and desperate. Two weeks of pent-up frustration and denial. Max's hands were on her hips and he gripped her so tightly she wondered dimly if the marks of his fingers would be on her flesh.

Darcy became aware of a noise after a few long seconds of letting Max suck her into a vortex of mindlessness and realised it was someone clearing his throat in a very obvious manner when she pulled back and was mortified to see a staff member—also mortified—waiting for them to come up for air.

Max released her hips from his grip and stood back. His hair was mussed, his tie awry. Darcy felt as if she might float away from the ground, she was so light-headed.

Max turned to face the red-faced staff member, who was obviously eager to pass on his message so he could escape.

'Sorry to disturb you, Signor Roselli, your car is ready when you are.'

The young man left and Darcy looked at Max, feeling stupid. 'Car? Where are we going?'

'The villa—Lake Como—for a long weekend.'

She must have looked as stupid as she felt.

'Our honeymoon?' he said.

Max had informed her a week before that they'd go away for a long weekend after the wedding, just so that everything looked as authentic as possible. She'd completely forgotten. Until now.

And suddenly the thought of a few days alone in a villa with Max was terrifying.

'Surely we can just stay here in Rome? There's so much to prepare for Scotland—' she gabbled.

Max was shaking his head and taking her hand to lead her back inside. 'We're going to Como, Darcy. Non-negotiable.'

He let go of her hand inside the door to the dining room and, as if sensing her growing desire to escape said firmly, 'Say goodbye to your parents, Darcy. I'll meet you in the foyer in an hour.'

She watched, still a little numb, as he strode over to some of the guests to start saying goodbye and felt a looming sense of futility wash over her. A weekend alone in a villa with Max Fonseca Roselli...after that kiss... She didn't stand a chance.

CHAPTER SEVEN

THE JOURNEY TO his private jet passed mainly in silence. Max had been waiting for Darcy in the lobby, as promised, and she'd been aware of every move he'd made in the car. Now, in the jet, he took a seat with graceful athleticism.

As much as she didn't want to attract his attention, it was hard to drag her eyes off him. He'd changed into dark trousers and a dark grey lightweight long-sleeved top that did little to disguise the sheer breadth and power of his chest. The grey of his top seemed to make his eyes burn more intensely, and Darcy looked away quickly, in case she was caught, as the small plane left the ground.

She'd changed too, into a 'going-away' outfit—a soft flowing knee-length sleeveless dress of dark cream with a matching jacket. Her hair was down and her scalp still prickled from the pins that had been holding it up, along with the veil.

She gently massaged her skull and thought of the poignant moment that had caught her unawares when she'd packed the dress and veil away in their boxes. She'd been thinking what a pity it was that she'd never have a daughter to hand it down to.

The stylist had seen her expression and said, 'Don't worry, Signora Roselli, we'll take good care of them for you.'

Hearing *Signora Roselli* had been enough to break her out of that momentary weakness and bring her back to reality. She was only Signora Roselli because Max craved world domination, and she—the fool—was helping him achieve it.

'For a new bride you're surprisingly quiet. Nervous about our wedding night, darling?'

Darcy cursed Max. If there was one mood in which he was pretty much irresisitible it was this more playful one that he so rarely displayed.

She glared at him and quirked a brow. 'I wouldn't know—not having much experience of being a new bride, and having even less inclination to be one ever again.'

Max tutted and smiled wolfishly. 'Don't worry, *dolcezza mia*, I'll be gentle with you.'

To Darcy's horror she felt herself getting hot, wondering what it would be like if this was *real* and Max was *really* promising to be gentle. She had an image of him with that intent look on his face as he thrust into her carefully, inch by inch… Between her legs she spasmed, her muscles reacting to her lurid imagination.

Horrified at her wayward body and, worse, at her desire to know what it would be like, she said curtly, 'Save it, Max. I'm not a virgin.'

She looked away when he said, 'So I don't need to be gentle, then? Good, because when we come together—'

Darcy snapped open her seatbelt and stood up, swaying a little as the plane hit some turbulence. She gripped the back of the seat to stay steady and said, 'I'm going to lie down. I'm tired.'

Max caught her wrist as she went past him and when she looked down he was frowning, all humour gone. 'What the hell, Darcy…? I'm just teasing you.'

She pulled her wrist free, already feeling like a prize idiot to have risen to such easy bait. 'I'm fine. I told you—I'm just tired. It's been a long day.'

She made her way to the small bedroom and slammed the door shut behind her, pressing the backs of her hands to hot cheeks. She cursed herself roundly as she paced back and forth. Of all the stupid— Why had she let Max wind her up like that?

She sat down on the edge of the bed, suddenly weary. Because the truth was that this whole day had got to her much more than she'd ever imagined it would, and his teasing had just highlighted that.

When she'd agreed to this marriage with Max she'd somehow believed that she could do it and remain relatively intact. Unscathed by the man.

But that had all been shot to hell. It had been shot to hell after that night in his office, when the true depth of her attraction to him had become painfully apparent.

Why did he have to find her attractive? This wasn't how the world worked—men like Max did *not* find women like Darcy attractive. She had no doubt that it was an aberration—a freakish anomaly. A desire borne out of the fact that she was so different from his usual type of woman. Stress-induced. Something-induced. But not real.

Her circling thoughts brought her back to one question: why had she followed that crazy instinct to apply for a job working for the man in the first place?

With a heartfelt groan Darcy flopped back onto the bed and shut her eyes, willing sleep to come and make her mind blissfully blank.

A sleek car was waiting for them when they arrived at the small airport just outside Milan. When their bags had been stowed Max sat in the driver's seat and Darcy got into the passenger side. The car was luxurious, and obviously high-end. When Max drove out of the airport it felt as if it was barely skimming the road.

He must have seen something of her appreciation because he said, 'This is the new Falcone road car. I'm friends with Rafaele—he lends me cars to test-drive every now and then.'

Darcy's mouth quirked, even though she was still wary after her outburst earlier. But she couldn't let Max see that he could get to her so easily. 'The perks of being friends with one of the world's most famous car manufacturers?'

Max shrugged lightly, wearing his mantle of

privilege easily. Darcy sighed. She couldn't even fault him for that, though. It wasn't as if he hadn't earned it.

'Darcy...' he said carefully. 'What happened earlier—'

She sat up and said quickly, 'It was nothing, really. It's just been a lot to take in.'

Max's hands clenched on the steering wheel and he said after a long moment, 'Do you know I've never really said thank you?'

She looked at him and his jaw was firm. He glanced at her, and then back to the road. 'Thank you, Darcy, for doing this. I don't underestimate how big a favour it is.'

Darcy felt herself weakening, any residual tendrils of anger fading. She knew Max well enough to know that he rarely said thank you unless it really meant something to him.

She was about to say something in response when an insidious suspicion occurred to her and her eyes narrowed on Max, taking in his oh, so benign expression in the half-light of the car. She folded her arms. 'I'm not sleeping with you, Max.'

He glanced at her again and that mocking look

was back on his face. 'I wasn't aware I'd asked the question.'

'You don't have to. It's there between us… But I just can't.'

Because you'll hurt me.

Darcy sucked in a breath, the truth finally revealing itself to her. She was in way too deep with Max already. If they slept together his inevitable rejection would crush her. The thought was utterly galling, but it was a fact.

Max's jaw was firm again in the low light of the car. 'I said before that I don't play games, Darcy. It's your choice.' He slid her a darkly wicked look. 'But I won't promise not to try to change your mind.'

In a firm bid to ignore that disturbing promise, Darcy changed the subject. 'Who owns the villa we're going to?'

'A good friend of mine and his family—Dante D'Aquanni.'

'I've heard of him,' Darcy said. 'He's in construction?'

Max nodded, negotiating a hairpin turn by the lake with skill. 'He and his family are living temporarily in Spain while he works on a project.'

'How do you know him?'

Max's hands tightened momentarily on the wheel. 'We go back a long way... He was one of the first clients I had who trusted me to invest his money for him.'

Precluding any further conversation, Max turned into a clearing where huge ornate gates loomed in the dark, with stone walls on either side. When the gates swung open Max drove in and a stunningly beautiful villa was revealed, with stone steps leading up to an impressive porch and door.

Golden light spilled from the doorway when it opened and a housekeeper came bustling out. A younger man joined the old woman who met them and took their bags. Max greeted the house-keeper warmly and introduced Darcy to the woman, who was called Julieta.

The D'Aquannis' housekeeper led them inside, chatting to Max easily, and Darcy guessed he'd been there before. The interior was awe-inspir-ing, with high ceilings, an impressive staircase, and huge rooms visible off the stone-flagged re-ception area.

One room, when Darcy peeked into it, seemed

to have a blue glass ceiling. Murano glass? she wondered.

Max turned to Darcy after Julieta had offered some refreshments and Darcy seized the opportunity to reply in front of a witness, saying in Italian that she was tired and would like to go to bed. She ignored Max's undoubtedly mocking look.

It was with a feeling of mounting dread, however, as they followed Julieta upstairs, that Darcy wondered if they were going to be shown to one bedroom...

To her abject relief Julieta opened a door, motioning to Max, and then led Darcy to the next door along the wide corridor, opening it to reveal a sumptuous bedroom with en suite bathroom and dressing room.

Julieta bustled off again, after pointing some things out to Darcy and telling her that breakfast would be ready at nine a.m.

Darcy's relief lasted precisely as long as it took for Max to appear in an adjoining doorway, with a wicked glint in his eye.

Arms folded across that broad chest, he leaned gracefully against the doorframe. 'I told Dante about the true nature of our marriage…needless to say I'm regretting that impulse now.'

Darcy put her hands on her hips. 'Well, I'm not. Goodnight, Max.'

Max said musingly, almost as if she hadn't spoken, 'You know, I've never really had to woo a woman before—I'm looking forward to it.'

Her belly exploded as if a hundred butterflies had been set free. Of *course* Max Fonseca Roselli Fonseca had never wooed a woman before, because they always fell into his lap like ripe plums.

She started walking towards the door, prepared to shut it in his face. 'I'll save you the trouble. I'm really not worth it.'

Max's gaze dropped down over her body with explicit directness. 'On the contrary…I think you'll be very worth it.' He stood away from the door then, and said, 'Goodnight, Darcy.'

And then the adjoining door closed in *her* face, before she could make a smart retort, and she looked at it feeling ridiculously deflated, curbing the urge to open it again and follow Max into his room.

What had she expected? That Max would ignore a challenge? She was very afraid that she'd handled this all wrong. Max would accept nothing less than total capitulation, and his tone of voice said that he didn't expect it to take all that long.

Darcy stomped around the thickly carpeted room, getting unpacked and ready for bed, and muttered to herself, 'Do your worst, Roselli. I'm stronger than you think.'

Apparently she wasn't as strong as she thought after all. When she emerged for breakfast the following morning and saw Max sitting at the table which had been set up on a terrace at the back of the villa she immediately felt weak.

She studiously ignored the spectacular view of the lake—she had a very old fear of any expanse of water, no matter how scenic it was.

Max was wearing worn jeans and a dark polo top, his hair dishevelled by the breeze. When he lifted his hand to take a sip from a small coffee cup his well-formed bicep bulged and Darcy went hot all over.

As if sensing her scrutiny, he looked up and smiled. 'Good morning...sleep well?'

She fixed a bright smile on her face and moved

forward, avoiding direct eye contact. 'Yes, thank you—like a baby and all people with a clear conscience.'

Max made an *ouch* sound and said dryly, 'Then I hate to inform you that I must be on the side of the angels as I slept well too.'

Darcy snorted inelegantly, helping herself to some pastries and pungent coffee, closing her eyes for a moment to savour the smell. *Heaven.*

When she opened them again it was to find Max giving her a leisurely once-over. His gaze stopped at her breasts and Darcy looked down, aghast to see the hard points of her nipples pushing against the thin material of the light sundress she'd put on, in the absence of anything remotely businesslike.

She resisted the urge to fold her arms over her chest and took her time over eating the delicious pastries and some fruit, avoiding Max studiously. When she did glance at him he seemed fixated on the corner of her mouth, and then he leaned forward to reach out and touch it with his index finger.

When he sat back she saw some jam on it, and he proceeded to lick it off the top of his finger—

which had a direct effect on the pulse between Darcy's legs and abruptly made her appetite fade to be replaced by a much earthier one.

Not willing to sit there like a mouse, while Max the predatory cat played with her, Darcy stood up and said briskly, 'I'll find out where the study is, shall I? And check e-mails and—'

Max stood up too and reached for Darcy easily, taking her hand. 'You're doing no such thing. I've got plans for today and they won't be taking place in a study.'

Darcy pulled free and stepped back, panic fluttering along her nerve-endings at the thought of Max devoting all his attention to her. 'I don't mind. We should really make sure that—'

Suddenly Max dipped out of sight and Darcy's world was upended. She found herself in his arms, clinging onto his neck in fright.

'What the hell—?' she got out in a choked voice.

But Max was saying something to Julieta over her head about being back later for dinner. The woman smiled at them benevolently, as if she saw this kind of thing all the time. It made Darcy wonder about the owners.

Max finally let her down once they were outside, in order to open the passenger door of the car. Darcy tried to make a dash for it, back to the villa, but he wound an arm around her waist, practically lifting her into the passenger seat.

Darcy fumed as she watched him come around the front of the car, his eyes on hers warning her not to defy him again. When he swung in and quickly locked the doors from the inside Darcy sputtered, 'This is tantamount to kidnap...and you're blatantly taking advantage of my size... You're a...a *sizeist*!'

Max was already driving smoothly out of the villa and he looked at her with dark amusement and said, 'I have to admit that your...portability makes you a little easier to control.'

Darcy made a strangled sound of outrage and crossed her arms over her chest, glaring out of the window as Max drove away from the villa. Damn him and his superior strength.

But while she hated the ease with which he was able to compel her to do his bidding all she could think about was how it had felt to be held so securely in his arms—how her instinct had been to burrow closer and seek a kind of refuge she'd never felt like seeking before. The fact that she could be as susceptible as the next woman to Max's caveman antics was not welcome.

Darcy only recognised where they were when she saw the signs for Milano. She turned to Max and said eagerly, 'You've come to your senses and we're going back to Rome to work?'

He quirked a half-smile. 'No. I'm taking you out.'

Out *where*, though? Darcy looked at him suspiciously but he gave nothing away.

And then he said, 'Apart from my very serious intention to get you into my bed, it'll be good for us to be seen together the weekend after our marriage. We *are* meant to be on honeymoon, after all.'

Darcy had no answer for that. He was right.

They parked in a private and exclusive car park with valet parking and emerged onto a busy Milan street that was bustling with weekend activity.

It was like a fashion parade, with beautiful women walking up and down—some with the requisite small dogs—and beautiful men… A little too metrosexual for Darcy, but then this was the fashion capital of Italy and arguably Europe. Predictably, Max stood out among these beautiful people and there were plenty of heads turning in recognition and appreciation.

After all, Darcy recalled, hadn't the Italians invented a word for walking around in order to be seen? *Passeggiata?*

Max took Darcy's hand in his and led her down the street. She wanted to pull away, but as if reading her mind he held on tight. Veering off to a small side street, Max ducked into a boutique with a world-famous designer's name over the door.

He was greeted like a superstar—and as a regular, Darcy noted with a dart of something dark. But before she could emit so much as a squeak she was whisked away behind a curtain and Max was left out in the foyer. At one stage she caught a glimpse of him sipping coffee and reading a newspaper.

She was completely bemused as industrious assistants flitted around her like exotic butterflies. Finally fitted into a stunning bodycon cocktail dress—a bit *too* bodycon for Darcy's taste—she was all but pushed back out onto the main salon floor. She realised she was being paraded for Max's benefit when he lowered his paper and looked her over as if she were a brood mare.

Anger started down low and then rose through her body in a tidal wave of heat and humiliation. She hissed at him, 'What the *hell* is this?'

His eyes snapped to hers. 'I'm taking you shopping.'

'I don't need any more clothes.'

Max looked nonplussed for a moment, as if he literally could not compute Darcy's reaction. It would have been funny if she hadn't been so angry. And what was making her even angrier was the evidence that this was obviously a regular occurrence for him…bringing women shopping.

So angry that she couldn't see straight, and feeling seriously constricted in the dress, she went straight to the door and walked out, almost tripping in the ridiculous heels. She was halfway down the street, with steam coming out of her ears, before Max caught up with her, standing in front of her to block her way easily.

'What the hell was *that*?'

'Exactly. What the hell *was* that? I thought you said you weren't used to wooing women? Does taking them shopping not count as wooing? Because evidently you do it a lot, going by your familiarity with those assistants in that shop—and quite a few others, I'd imagine.'

Max threw his hands up in the air. 'What woman doesn't love shopping?'

Darcy pointed a finger at herself. 'This one.' Then she folded her arms, her eyes narrowed on him. 'Maybe you consider taking women shopping as foreplay?'

They glowered at each other for a long moment, and then Max sighed deeply and put his hands on his hips. Eventually he muttered something like, 'Should have known better...'

Darcy put a hand behind her ear. 'Sorry? What was that?'

Max looked at her and his mouth twitched ever so slightly. He said, with exaggerated precision, 'I'm sorry for assuming you would want to go shopping. I should have known better.'

Darcy's own mouth was tempted to twitch, but she curbed the urge. 'Yes, you should. And I can't breathe in this dress.'

Max's gold gaze dropped and took her in, and then he said roughly, 'I don't think *I* can breathe with you in that dress.'

Immediately Darcy's brain started to overheat and she was in danger of forgetting why she was angry.

Max put out his hand. 'Come on—let's take it back.'

With her hand in his, walking back down the street, Darcy felt a little foolish for storming out like a petulant child. That wasn't her. She winced. But it *was* her around Max. He just wound her up. After all, he'd only been doing what he'd thought would make her happy.

She squeezed his hand and he looked at her just before they got to the shop. 'I'm sorry. I just... I'm not that into shopping. It's not that I'm not grateful.'

Max gave her a wry grin. 'I didn't exactly go about it with any finesse. Come on.'

He pushed the door open and a very sheepish Darcy walked in behind him, mortified under the speculative gazes of the staff.

When she was dressed in her own clothes she breathed a sigh of relief, and when she was out in the main part of the shop again she spied a bright, colourful scarf and took it to the till.

Immediately Max was there to pay for it. Darcy glared at him, but he ignored her and she sighed. When they were outside she tucked the scarf into her bag and he looked at her expressively. Feeling defensive, she said, 'Well, I felt like I had to buy *something*!'

Max rolled his eyes and said dryly, 'Believe me, those saleswomen are like piranhas.'

Darcy sniffed. 'I just felt bad, that's all.'

Max took her hand and Darcy glanced up. He was looking at her with a funny expression on his face. 'You've got a good heart, Darcy Lennox.'

She snorted, but inwardly fluttered. 'Hardly.'

And then, just as they were passing another boutique—much smaller but no less exclusive—Darcy stopped in her tracks. The dress in the window was exquisite—off the shoulder, deep royal blue satin, with a scooped neck and a boned bodice that would accentuate an hourglass figure.

When Darcy realised what she was doing she grew hot with embarrassment and went to keep walking, but Max stopped her, an incredulous look on his face.

'And you call *me* mercurial?'

Darcy smiled weakly. 'I didn't say I *hate* shopping. I'm like a heat-seeking missile—once I see what I want I go for it and then get out again.'

'*Do* you want it?' he asked.

Darcy squirmed. 'Well…I like it…' She looked at it wistfully.

Max pulled her into the shop and this time paced the small space while she tried the dress on, together with suitable underwear and shoes.

The assistant stood back and said appreciatively, *'Bella figura, signora.'*

Max appeared at the dressing room door, clearly a little bored. When his eyes widened Darcy's heart-rate zoomed skywards.

'Is it okay?' she asked shyly. And then she babbled, 'You know, I probably do need a dress for the Montgomerys' party, so…'

'We'll take it.' Max's voice sounded slightly constricted.

Once Max had arranged for the dress and sundries to be sent to his office in Rome they left again. Darcy had tried to pay for the dress but of course he hadn't let her.

Back out in the sunshine, he looked at her and said, almost warily, 'What now?'

Darcy looked around, enjoying seeing Max knocked slightly off his confident stride. 'Well, first I want some gelato...'

Max's eyes boggled. 'After you've just bought that dress?' And then he shook his head. *'Incredibile.'*

Smiling now, he took her hand and pressed a kiss to the palm. Darcy looked around surreptitiously for paparazzi, but couldn't see any obvious cameras pointed at them.

'And after the gelato?'

She screwed up her nose and thought. 'Well, I've never seen *The Last Supper* by Leonardo Da Vinci, so that'd be nice, and I'd like to walk on the roof of the Duomo and see if we can see the Alps.' Darcy looked at Max. 'What about you?'

Max blinked. What about *him*? No one had ever asked him before what *he'd* like to do. And the fact that he'd assumed for a second that he could just take Darcy shopping— He shook his head mentally now at his lack of forethought. But he hadn't been thinking—he'd just wanted to get them out of the villa before she could lock herself in the study.

Clearly, though, he'd underestimated her and would need to be far more inventive. For the first time in a long time Max felt the thrill of a challenge and something else—something almost... *light*.

'Do you know what I'd like?'

She shook her head.

'To go and see the AC Milan game.'

Darcy looked at her watch and then said impishly, 'Well, then, you're going to have your work cut out making sure we fit it all in, aren't you?'

'That last goal...' Darcy shook her head and trailed off.

Max glanced at her, sitting in the passenger seat. They were almost back at the villa and he couldn't remember a day he'd enjoyed as much.

They'd stood before one of the great artworks of the world and then climbed to the top of a magnificent cathedral to see the spectacular view. They hadn't seen the snowy Alps through the heat haze that hung over the city, much to Darcy's disappointment, and it had made Max feel an absurd urge to fix that for her. And they'd been to a football match. He *never* got to go to see his favourite team play. He was always too busy.

He teased Darcy. 'So you're a fan of AC Milan now?'

She looked at him and grinned. 'I could get used to it. I never realised football was so gladiatorial. My father's a rugby man, so I grew up being dragged to rugby matches. Whatever country we were in I found it was a way of orientating myself, because we moved around so much.'

Max found himself thinking of something that had nagged at him, and asked curiously, 'Does that have anything to do with the very specific amount of money you requested?'

Darcy went still, but then she wrinkled her nose and said lightly, 'Isn't it a little crass to talk about money with your fake wife?'

Max shook his head. 'You're not avoiding the question so easily. You should have asked for a different amount. Ever heard of rounding up?'

Darcy scowled, making Max even more determined to know what the money was for. He would have given it to her in bonuses anyway, but the fact that she'd asked for it...

She sighed, and then said, 'When my folks split up they sold the family home. They never really settled again. I went to boarding school, my dad was travelling all over the world, and my mother was wherever her newest lover was. When my father's business fell apart and I went back to the UK to a comprehensive school it was my most settled time—even if we were living out of a cheap hotel.'

She shrugged.

'I've just always wished that I had somewhere… somewhere that I knew would always be there.' She let some hair slip forward, covering her face, and muttered, 'It's silly, really. I mean, lots of people don't have a home at all—'

Max reached out and put his hand over hers. 'It's not silly.'

He couldn't say any more because he knew exactly what Darcy was talking about. He'd never had that safe centre either.

He took his hand away to change gears. 'So, the money—it's for a house?'

Darcy nodded and smiled, not looking at him. 'It's a small flat in London. I've been keeping my eye on it for a few months now.'

Max could see Darcy all too easily—stepping out of a cute little flat on a leafy street, getting on with her life, disappearing into the throng of people. And he wasn't sure he liked it at all. In fact, if he wasn't mistaken, the flare of dark heat in his gut felt suspiciously like jealousy.

When Darcy had freshened up and changed into comfortable loose trousers and a silk top she went downstairs to dinner. It was set up on the terrace, in the lingering twilight. Flickering candles lent everything a golden glow and the opulent rugs and furnishings made her wonder about the couple who were lucky enough to own this idyll. Did they have a happy marriage? Somehow, Darcy thought they must, because there was an air of quiet peace about the place.

And then she shook herself mentally. She wasn't usually prone to such flights of the imagination.

Max wasn't there yet and she breathed a sigh of relief, going to the stone wall and looking out over the dark expanse of the lake at the lights coming on on the other side.

Even here, far away from the water, she felt it like a malevolent presence and shuddered lightly.

'Cold?'

Darcy whirled around, her heart leaping into her throat, to see Max holding out a glass of wine. She took it quickly, ducking her head. 'No, I'm fine...just a ghost walking over my grave.'

She sneaked a look at him as he stood beside her. He'd changed too, into dark trousers and a white shirt which inevitably made his dark skin stand out even more. He oozed casual elegance, and yet with that undeniable masculine edge that made him all man.

The day they'd spent together had passed in an enjoyable blur of sights and sounds, but mostly Max had been a revelation. Darcy had never seen him so relaxed or easygoing. As if a weight had been lifted off his shoulders.

At the football match he'd been like a little boy—jumping up and down with the crowd, embracing her and the man next to him when his team scored. Also spouting language that had shocked her when things hadn't gone well.

Julieta and the young man who it had turned out was her grandson delivered their dinner: fragrant plates of pasta to start, and then a main course of tender pork in a traditional sundried tomato, prosciutto and sage sauce.

Darcy groaned appreciatively when she tasted the delicious pork and said wryly, 'I may have to be rolled out of here in a couple of days.'

Max looked at her, and his gaze running over her curves told her exactly what he thought of that. Unused to being appreciated for what she normally considered to be a drawback, she avoided his eye again. A part of her still couldn't really believe he wanted her, but all day he'd touched her with subtle intention, keeping her on a knife-edge of desire.

In a bid to try and pierce this bubble of intimacy that surrounded them on the terrace, with the sound of the lake lapping not far away, Darcy asked about the couple who owned the house. 'I just wondered what they're like. This seems to be a happy place.'

Max pushed his empty plate away and then stood up, saying, 'I'll show you a picture.'

He returned a couple of minutes later with a beaming Julieta, who was dusting a picture with her apron. She handed it to Darcy. It showed an insanely handsome dark man, smiling widely, with a very petite blonde woman whose hair was a mass of crazy curls. She was also grinning, and holding a young boy with dark hair by the hand, while the man held a toddler high in his arms— a little girl with dark curly hair, a thumb stuck firmly in her mouth, eyes huge.

Something lanced Darcy deep down. This was a picture of familial happiness that she only knew as a distant dream. And who was to say that they wouldn't split up, with those poor children destined to spend a lifetime torn between two parents?

Aghast that she was even thinking of this in the face of such evident joy, she handed the picture back quickly with a fixed smile. 'They're lovely.'

Julieta took the picture away, carefully cleaning it again. She obviously missed them. She must be more like a member of the family than a housekeeper to them, Darcy guessed.

Max said into the silence, 'Perhaps not everyone goes through what we experienced.'

Darcy looked at him, wondering why she was surprised he'd read her mind. It seemed to be a speciality of his. 'Do you really believe that?'

He smiled and shook his head. 'Personally? No.

But I have to admit that Dante and Alicia seem very…happy.' And then he asked abruptly, 'Why did you step in that day? During the fight?'

Darcy knew immediately that Max was referring to what she'd witnessed at Boissy, when she'd intervened. The memory of how exposed she'd felt after doing it made her squirm now. 'I can't believe you remember that.'

Max's mouth tipped up at one corner. 'It was pretty memorable. You single-handedly scared off three guys who were all easily three times your size.'

Max took her hand in his and hers looked tiny. It made her too aware of their inherent differences.

She shrugged. 'I just…saw them…and I didn't really think, to be honest.' She bit her tongue to stop herself from revealing that she'd used to watch Max far too intently, far too aware of his presence. Aware of the insolence he'd worn like a shield.

Afraid that he might see it, she deflected the conversation back onto him.

'You and your brother…do you think you'll ever be close?'

Darcy thought he'd pull his hand away, but he left it there, holding hers.

Quietly, he said, 'We used to be close. Before we were separated. Closer than anyone.' He looked at Darcy and smiled. 'We had a special language. It used to drive our parents crazy.' And then the smile faded. 'Luca was stronger than me, though...older by a few minutes. When our parents told us they were taking one each he just stood there—not crying, not saying anything. I'll never forget it.' Max's mouth twisted. 'I was the one that fell apart.'

Darcy turned her hand in Max's and gripped it. A sense of rage at his parents filled her, shocking in its intensity. 'You were little more than a baby, Max...'

Just then Julieta appeared, with a coffee pot on a tray, and Darcy blinked up at her, broken out of the web of intimacy that had come down over her and Max without her even realising it. Suddenly she felt very raw, and absurdly emotional. The full impact of the day was hitting her. She was in danger of losing herself out here with Max.

Acting on impulse, she seized the opportunity like a coward, pulling her hand back from Max's, avoiding his eye. She stood up, smiled, and said, 'No coffee for me, thanks—it's been a long day.'

Unfortunately she couldn't quite manage to leave at the same time as Julieta because Max had caught her wrist. Darcy looked down and her heart skipped a beat. To her intense relief his expression indicated nothing of their recent conversation. He looked altogether far too sexy and dangerous. Far too reminiscent of that younger Max—cocky and confident, but still human underneath it all.

He smiled, and it was the smile of a shark. 'You're not willing to concede defeat yet?'

Darcy shook her head and struggled against the blood that pounded in her veins. 'No, Max, I still don't think it's a good idea.'

To her surprise he let her go and leaned forward to pour himself some coffee. '*Buonanotte*, then, Darcy...'

Feeling unsure, because she didn't trust Max an inch, Darcy sidled around him to get to the doorway.

And then she heard him say softly, 'It's better that you go to bed now because you'll need your sleep. I'll be waking you early in the morning. I've got more plans for tomorrow.'

She looked at him suspiciously. 'What are you talking about?'

He just smiled and said, 'You'll see.'

Darcy started to speak. 'Look, Max—'

He speared her a look that told her in no uncertain terms that he was hanging on to his control by a thread and that if she stayed a moment longer he wouldn't be responsible for his actions.

'Goodnight, Darcy. Go to bed while you still can...or it won't be alone.'

She had the sense not to ask anything else and fled.

CHAPTER EIGHT

'LEMME ALONE. IT'S the middle of the night.' Darcy burrowed back into the bed as deep as she could, but big firm hands reached in determinedly and ripped the covers back.

She squealed, wide awake now, and looked at Max looming over her, in the *very* early morning gloom.

'Buongiorno, mia moglie.' My wife.

Darcy scowled, feeling thoroughly disgruntled and aware that she was in just skimpy pants and a vest top.

She scrabbled for a sheet but Max insisted on pulling it back again, saying briskly, 'Now, I can dress you, or you can dress yourself—it's up to you. I've laid some clothes out for you.'

There was enough light in the room for a squinting Darcy to see that Max was wide awake, dressed casually, and that those mesmerising eyes were making a very thorough and leisurely appraisal of her body.

Then he said throatily, '*If*, on the other hand, you'd prefer to stay in bed, I won't object.'

Her body jumped with anticipation but she ignored it and scrambled off the bed, reaching for a robe. 'I'm up.' She rounded on him, saying grumpily, 'And I can dress myself.'

Max made a considering noise. 'Not a morning person? I'll make a note to prepare myself for that in the future.'

'It'd be more accurate to say not a middle of the night person,' Darcy snapped.

Max was thankfully backing away, and he glanced at his watch, saying, 'Downstairs in fifteen minutes. We've time for a quick breakfast.'

Darcy grumbled about arrogant bossy men as she washed and got dressed in jeans and a pretty silk long-sleeved top, shoving her feet into flat shoes.

She didn't like to admit that her defences still felt a little battered after yesterday and their intimate supper last night. She'd had disturbing dreams of small boys clinging onto each other as unseen hands forced them apart, and of bright red blood on pristine snow.

When she went down she was surprised to see Julieta up and about, greeting her with a cheery hello. She showed her to a covered part of the terrace at the back of the villa, clearly in deference to the fact that only the faintest trails of dawn could be seen in the sky, like delicate pink ribbons.

Max was drinking coffee. He looked at her and stood to pull out a chair.

Darcy felt exposed, with her freshly scrubbed face and her hair tied back in a ponytail. She valiantly tried to ignore Max and picked at a croissant and some fruit, still feeling fuzzy from sleep.

'You're not going to tell me where we're going, are you?'

Max shook his head cheerfully. 'It's a surprise.'

Darcy was already reacting to the prospect of another day in close proximity to Max… Her body was humming with energy.

She pushed her plate back, having no appetite this early, and said, 'I suppose now is as good a time as any to tell you I hate surprises?'

She did, too, having learnt long ago that they were usually of the very unwelcome variety—more often than not something promised by one or other of her parents to assuage their guilt or to compensate for their absence at some event or other.

Hence carving out a steady, dependable career for herself, where no surprises would jump out to get her.

Until she'd agreed to this ridiculous charade.

Max stood up and put down his napkin. 'You'll like it—I promise. Ready?'

Darcy looked up and sighed inwardly at the determination stamped on his face. 'I don't have much choice, do I?'

He shook his head. 'Not unless you want me to put you over my shoulder and carry you out.'

Darcy had no doubt that Max wouldn't hesitate to put her over his shoulder—after all, he'd picked her up as if she was a bag of flour yesterday.

She stood up with as much grace as she could muster and said witheringly, 'You don't have to demonstrate your he-man capabilities again. I can walk.'

* * *

They drove a relatively short distance to a big flat open field, with several low buildings inside the gates. Max parked the car alongside some other vehicles and got out.

When she met him in front of the car, thoroughly bemused, he handed her something. 'Here, you'll need this—it might be a bit chilly.'

She took the fleece and guessed it must belong to the lady of the villa, because it fitted her perfectly and she'd looked to be about as petite as Darcy—if not smaller. Darcy zipped it up, suddenly glad of the extra layer against Max's far too intense perusal.

He'd put on a fleece too, and now took a basket from the boot of the car. Determined not to give Max the satisfaction of knowing how curious she was, Darcy just followed him around one of the low hangar-like buildings—and then stopped in her tracks and gasped out loud.

As she took in the significance of the scene in front of her she could feel the last of her defences crumble to dust. And, absurdly, tears pricked her eyes.

Max had stopped and was looking at her, the

picture of innocence. Darcy curled her hands into fists at her sides and glared at him, willing the emotion to stay down.

In a husky voice she said, 'Of all the low-down, dirty, manipulative things to do, Max Fonseca Roselli…this just proves how cold-hearted you are.'

It was a hot air balloon, on its side, being inflated by a crew.

And it was on her bucket list.

One night, while working late in the office in that first couple of months, Darcy had asked Max idly about what might be on *his* bucket list—because what could someone who had nearly everything possibly want?

He'd given her a typical non-answer, in true evasive Max style. And then he'd asked her what was on hers. She'd replied, with some measure of embarrassment, that she'd always wanted to take a hot air balloon ride.

And now he was giving it to her.

Emotion tightened her chest.

Max just looked amused. 'You don't want to go?'

She glared at him. 'Of *course* I want to go.'

She folded her arms across her chest, hating it that he could make her *feel* so much, wanting to extract some kind of payment.

'But I'm not going anywhere until you tell me what's on *your* bucket list. And I want a proper answer this time.'

Max's expression hardened. 'I don't have a bucket list. This is ridiculous, Darcy. We'll miss the best part of the sunrise if we don't move now.'

She could see the balloon, lifting into the air behind Max. She tapped her foot. Waiting...

He sighed deeply and ran a hand through his hair impatiently. 'Nothing with you comes easy, does it?'

'No.' She smiled sweetly, feeling some measure of satisfaction to be annoying him—especially when he'd hauled her out of bed so early.

'Okay, I'll tell you—but you're not to laugh.'

Darcy shook her head and said seriously, 'I promise I won't.'

Max looked up, as if committing his soul somewhere—or hers, more likely—and then down again, and said in a rush, 'I want to own a football club.'

He'd said it like a young boy, blurting something out before he could lose his nerve, and Darcy's chest squeezed even tighter.

She pushed the emotion down and nodded once. 'Thank you. Now we can go,' she said.

Once she felt on a more even keel with Max she was like a child, with the full excitement of what he'd organised for her—whatever his motive—finally hitting her.

They were helped into the basket alongside the pilot, and then suddenly they were lifting off the ground and into the clear dawn-streaked sky. Darcy wrapped her hands tight around the basket's edge, eyes wide at the way the ground dropped away beneath them.

It was pure terror and exhilaration. Max stood beside her as the pilot edged them higher and higher, but she couldn't look at him, too afraid of what he might see on her face.

Time and time again her father had promised to do this with her and it had never happened. And now she was here with her husband. Except he wasn't really her husband.

Emotions twisted like a ball in her gut and she took a deep breath.

Max's hand covered hers. 'Okay?'

When she felt more in control she looked at him and smiled. 'Perfect.'

The balloon made lazy progress over the spectacular countryside, with the pilot pointing out Lake Como and the other lakes. Far in the distance they saw the snowy tips of the Alps. Milan was a dark blur in the distance as they passed over fields and agricultural lands.

Darcy was entranced. When the gas wasn't firing, to propel the balloon higher, she thought she'd never experienced such peace and solitude.

When she could, she tore her eyes from the view and looked at Max. 'Is this your first time in a balloon too?'

He nodded and smiled, leaning one elbow on the basket-edge. Darcy had the uncomfortable sensation that he'd been looking at her and not the view. And she hated it that she was relieved he hadn't done this with anyone else.

She teased him now. 'You're not twitching at being so far from communication and Montgomery?'

Max lifted his phone out of his pocket and held it up to show that it had no bars of service, then put it back. 'Nope.'

He sounded inordinately cheerful about the fact, and Darcy marvelled again at this far more relaxed Max.

The view filled her eyes so much that it almost hurt as the sky got lighter and lighter, exploding into shades of vivid pink and red as the sun came up over the Alps in the distance.

She didn't notice that Max had been doing anything until he produced a glass of sparkling wine for her and another for himself. He offered one to the pilot, who smiled but declined.

Max clinked his glass off hers and then the view was blotted out as his mouth came over hers and she fell deep into a spinning vortex that had only a little bit to do with the fact that they were suspended above the earth in a floating balloon.

Only their mouths were touching, but Darcy felt as if his hands were moving over her naked flesh. When Max pulled back she had to grip the edge of the basket tight, afraid she might just float off into the sky altogether. She was telling herself desperately that it had only been for the benefit of the pilot. To keep up appearances.

She took a sip of the wine and the bubbles exploded down her throat and into her belly. She couldn't be more intoxicated right now than if she'd drunk three bottles in quick succession.

They sipped their wine and gazed over the view in companionable silence. Every now and then the pilot pointed something out, or Max asked him a question about the balloon's mechanics.

Darcy hadn't even realised she was shivering lightly until Max came and took her empty glass and moved behind her, wrapping his arms around her, his hands over hers.

She settled into the hard cocoon of his body far too easily. Stripped bare by the experience. His fingers entwined with hers and his head bent and he feathered a hot kiss to her exposed neck. She shivered again, but this time it wasn't because of the cold.

They stood like that for a long time, and then the pilot said something low to Max and she felt him take in a breath behind her. Even though she knew what he was going to say, she didn't want it to end.

'We have to turn back... The air is starting to warm up...'

Darcy was glad he couldn't see her face. Tears stung her eyes but she said lightly, 'Okay.'

The ride back seemed to pass in a flash, and all too soon they were descending and the ground was rushing to meet them. They landed with a soft thud and a small bounce before the crew grabbed the basket and held it upright while they got out.

Max got out first and then lifted Darcy into his arms. For a moment he didn't put her down. Something in his eyes held her captive. And then she realised they had an audience and she blushed and scrambled down.

She went to the pilot and pressed an impetuous kiss to his cheek. 'I know you must be used to it—but, truly, that was magical. Thank you.'

The man looked pleased, but embarrassed, and said gruffly, 'You never get used to it. *Grazie*, Signora Roselli.'

Max took her by the hand, and as they walked to the car Darcy was aware that she'd made a decision. It was as if the balloon ride's unique perspective on the earth had shown her an eagle eye view of just how fragile life looked from above…how silly she was being not to reach out and grab precious moments, no matter how finite they might be.

The thought of continuing to deny herself after what she'd just experienced made her feel panicky—as if something incredibly precious might slip out of her grasp for ever. She didn't care about the consequences.

Max stopped at the car and faced her. He had a look of resolute determination on his face. 'Ready for the next part of the surprise?'

Darcy looked at him. She wouldn't put it past him to have organised something like a trip to Venice for the day... But she shook her head and said clearly, 'No more surprises.'

A range of expressions crossed Max's face: irritation, disappointment, renewed determination...

She took a breath. 'I don't mean what you think I mean. I'm wooed, Max. I don't even really care if that balloon ride was a purely cynical move on your part, I loved it too much and thank you for planning it. And I'm done fighting you. I want you. Take me back to the villa.'

Max wasn't sure how he drove in a straight line back to the villa. He kept Darcy's hand in his and the journey was made in silence, with the mounting anticipation coursing through his body saturating the air between them.

When he glanced at Darcy he could see a similar kind of tension on her small face and it only made his blood flow hotter. *Dio*. He wanted this woman so badly. More than he'd ever wanted anything.

Some kind of warning prickled over his skin at that assertion, but he ignored it.

She'd accused him of being cynical in his decision to organise the hot air balloon ride and he might have been…before. But he'd only thought of it the previous day, when they'd stood on the roof of the Duomo in Milan and she'd been disappointed not to see the Alps.

Max had remembered Dante talking about taking a hot air balloon ride with his family and seeing the Alps, and at the same time Max had recalled Darcy mentioning it some months ago.

In truth, the experience had moved him far more profoundly than he would ever have expected. He'd never seen the earth from above like that when not encased in a plane, with stacks of facts and figures in front of him, hurtling towards yet another meeting to shore up his funds, his reputation. That had all felt dangerously in-consequential when floating soundlessly through the sky.

Max was aware of the fact that this marriage to Darcy was not proceeding at all the way he might have expected when he'd first proposed the idea...the means to his end were veering way off the track. But right now he couldn't care less. All he cared about was Darcy and the fact that she would be *his*.

When they got back to the villa it was early af-ternoon. Darcy knew she should be feeling hun-gry because she hadn't had much breakfast, but she was only hungry for one thing: Max. Now that she'd decided to stop fighting him—and her-self—the full extent of her desire was unleashed and it was fearsome.

He held her hand as they went into the villa and Julieta greeted them, clearly surprised to see them back early—evidently Max *had* had more plans for the day, but Darcy was too keyed up to care what they might have been.

She heard him say to Julieta that she could take the rest of the weekend off if there were some provisions in the kitchen. The housekeeper only lived in the gate lodge nearby, but still Darcy's face burned with embarrassment, as if it was glaringly obvious what they intended to do.

But the woman took her leave cheerfully, after extracting a promise that they'd ring if they needed anything. Evidently she was used to such instructions.

Once she was gone, and the villa had fallen silent around them, Darcy looked at Max. Within seconds she was in his arms, their mouths fused, desperation clawing up from somewhere…the deepest, hottest part of her.

After long, drugging kisses and shedding outer layers they broke apart, and Max said gutturally, 'I'm not taking you here in the hall.'

Before she could object he'd picked her up in his arms, taken the stairs two at a time and shouldered his way into his bedroom. Sunlight streamed in the window and bathed Max in a golden glow. Never more so than now had he looked so awe-inspiring, and Darcy had to push down the quiver of self-doubt that he really desired her at all.

He put her on her feet and reached behind him

to pull his top over his head. His chest was bare and right in front of her face. Wide and muscled. Lean. Dark golden hair dusting the surface.

Darcy wasn't sure if she was breathing—but she was still upright, so she must be. She reached out a tentative hand and touched him, hearing his indrawn breath as her nail scraped a nipple.

He cupped her jaw and tipped her chin up. Dark colour slashed his cheekbones. She could see the question in his eyes and was surprised—she'd have expected him to take ruthless advantage of her acquiescence, giving her no time to change her mind.

To stop the rise of dangerous emotions, and before he could say anything, she put her hand over his mouth. 'I know who you are, I know who I am, and I know what I want—and that's you.'

She felt shaky. That was about as close as she could get to telling Max that she was perfectly aware that he'd move on once he'd had her but she was okay with that. If she didn't want him so badly right now she might hate herself for grinding her self-respect into the dust.

The question faded from Max's eyes and he put his hands to the bottom of her top, lifting it up.

She raised her arms and it slipped up and over her head. Next Max pulled free the band holding her hair, so that it feathered down over her shoulders.

His gaze dropped to the swells of her breasts, encased in lace. *'Bella...'* His voice was thick.

Darcy reached around behind her and undid her bra, letting it slip to the floor. She groaned softly when Max reverently cupped her breasts, pushing the voluptuous mounds together, rough thumbs making her nipples spring to attention, tight with need. She'd never felt so grateful for her curves as she did right then.

Her hands were busy on his jeans, undoing the top button. Warm flesh and his hard lower belly contracted against her fingers. It was heady to know she could do this to him.

He'd lowered his head and was exploring her with his hot mouth, his wicked tongue flicking against her breasts, learning the shape of her and the way her flesh quivered and tightened at his touch.

Darcy's hands were clumsy as she ripped free buttons and felt the potent hard bulge of him against her knuckles. Eventually she was able to push down his jeans over lean hips, but then she had to stop because Max had one of her nipples between his teeth, teasing it gently before letting it go to suck the fleeting pain away.

Her legs wouldn't hold her up any more and she fell back onto the bed. Max stood tall, his chest moving rapidly with his breath. He pushed his jeans down the rest of the way, and then his briefs, and Darcy's eyes widened on his impressive erection.

Her mouth watered, and when Max bent over to undo her jeans and pull them down she lifted her hips to help him. She felt only mounting impatience as he looked her over with possessive heat, pulling her panties off to join her jeans on the floor. No teenage crush could have prepared her for this reality. She felt as if she was burning up from the inside out as her hungry gaze roved over Max's perfect form, every muscle hard and honed.

A broad chest tapered down to lean hips, where his masculinity was long and thick, cradled between his strong thighs, long legs. He truly was a warrior from another time.

The ache between her own legs intensified and

she widened them in a tacit plea, not even really aware of what she was doing, knowing only that she craved this man deep in her core—*now.*

Max cursed softly and reached into his bedside console for something. Protection. He smoothed it onto his length and then came down over Darcy, an arm under her back, arching her up, mouths fused, tongues duelling. Her breasts were crushed against his chest and she was arching into him, begging…

Max pulled away for a second. 'I need you, Darcy… The first time I can't do slow.'

She felt as if she was caught in the grip of something elemental. 'I don't want slow. I need you too—*now.*'

For an infinitesimal moment everything seemed to be suspended, and then he thrust into her in one smooth move, so deep that Darcy gasped, and her back arched at this invasion of her flesh, ready as she was.

Max stopped. '*Dio*…have I hurt you? You're so small…'

'No,' said Darcy fiercely, wrapping her legs around him as far as they'd go. 'Don't stop…'

The initial sting of pain was fading. She'd never

felt so stretched, so full. And as Max moved his big body in and out she felt a deep sense of peace bloom and grow within her even as intense excitement built and built, until all her muscles were shaking with the effort it took to hold on against the rising storm.

Max put a hand between them, unerringly finding her centre and touching her there. 'You first, Darcy…then I'll fall…'

Darcy looked deep into his eyes, locked onto them tight as she finally relinquished her control to this man and fell so hard and so fast that she blacked out for a moment. She only came back to her dulled senses when Max's heavy body slumped over hers, their breathing harsh and ragged in the quiet room.

When the sky was tinged with the dying rays of the sun outside they made love again. Slowly, taking the time to learn everything they hadn't had time to do the first time around. Hands slipped and glided, squeezed and gripped. Max's fingers explored, feeling the telltale slickness between Darcy's legs, needing no more encouragement. He wrapped his hand around the back of Darcy's thigh and lifted it so that he could deepen his thrust into her body. He groaned with sheer pleasure that she held him so snugly.

She smoothed back the hair from his forehead, her hands gripping his shoulders, urging him on. It was a long, slow dance, building and building to a crescendo that broke over them, taking Max by surprise with its intensity.

When he had the strength to move he scooped Darcy against his front, with her knees drawn up so her buttocks were cupped in his lap. Wrapping his arms tight around her, he felt his mind blank of anything but a delicious feeling of satisfaction, and slipped into oblivion.

When Darcy woke it was dark outside. She had no sense of time or space for a disorientating moment, not recognising the room she was in. And then she moved, and winced as muscles—intimate muscles—protested.

Max. His big body thrusting so deep that she'd been unable to hold back a hoarse cry of pleasure… It all rushed back. The desperation of that first coupling, followed by that lengthy, luxurious exploration. Her skin felt sensitive, tenderised.

She sat up now, looking around the moonlit room. No sounds from the bathroom. Moving to the side of the bed, Darcy stood up, wincing slightly again, and reached for the robe left on the end of the bed.

She opened the door and immediately a mouth-watering smell hit her nostrils. She followed it instinctively, realising just how hungry she was as she stumbled to a halt in the doorway of the kitchen.

Max was stirring something in a pot, humming tunelessly, wearing low slung sweat pants and a T-shirt.

'Hey…' Darcy hovered at the door, feeling ridiculously self-conscious.

Max turned around and looked her over, those dark eyes gleaming with something she couldn't read.

'Ciao.'

Darcy came further in. 'What time is it?'

'About three in the morning. You must be starving.'

There was a very wicked gleam in Max's eyes and Darcy fought back an urge to poke her tongue out at that and at his far too smug look. She was ravenous. Not that she'd admit it.

She shrugged a shoulder, feigning nonchalance. 'A little, I guess.'

'Liar,' Max said easily, and came around the kitchen island to scoop her up against him and kiss away any faux nonchalance for good.

He let her go and walked back around to the pot.

Darcy was dizzy. 'What are you cooking?' she managed to get out over her palpitating heart. That kiss had told her that they were nowhere near finished with this mutual...whatever it was...

'Pasta with *funghi porcini* in a creamy white wine sauce.'

Max had dished up the pasta now, into two bowls, and was bringing them over to a rustic table. He brought over some bread, and a bottle of wine and two glasses.

Darcy came over, mouth watering. When she took a bite the *al dente* pasta and its flavours exploded on her tongue. It all felt incredibly decadent—as if this were some kind of illicit midnight feast.

After finishing her pasta, Darcy took a long luxurious sip of wine and asked idly, 'So what was the other part of the surprise that we missed today?'

Max sat back, cradling his own glass of wine, and smirked at her. 'I don't think you deserve to know.'

Darcy dipped her fingers in her water glass and flicked some at him. 'That's *so* unfair.' She mock pouted. 'I put out before you even had to go through with it.'

Max gave her a considering look full of mischief. 'That's true. If I'd known how easy it would be—'

Now Darcy scooped up a much larger handful of water and threw it at him. An incredible lightness infused her as Max put down his glass and smiled devilishly at her. He still managed to look gorgeous, even as water dripped down his face and onto his chest.

He picked up his own glass of water and looked at her explicitly.

She gasped and got up from her chair, inching away from him. 'You wouldn't dare…'

But he would. Of course he would.

Max stood up and advanced on her as Darcy fled behind the kitchen island.

'Max, stop—we're adults, and this isn't our kitchen.' She was attempting to sound reasonable, but the breathiness in her voice gave her away.

He raised a brow. 'It's only water, Darcy. Now, come here like a good girl. You can't tease me and expect to get away with it.'

Darcy crept around the island as Max followed her and eyed where the door was. When she made her move, feinting left before going towards the door, Max caught her with pathetic ease, grabbing her robe and pulling her into him.

He captured her hands with one of his and pulled her up against him. She caught fire. He was walking her backwards towards the huge table, and illicit excitement leapt in Darcy's blood. She didn't *play* like this. And she suspected Max didn't either. It was heady.

The back of the table hit her buttocks and Max nudged her until she was sitting on it. He still held the full glass of water over her and he said in a rough voice, 'Open your robe.'

A sliver of self-consciousness pricked her. 'Max…' she said weakly.

'Open it, Darcy, or I'll open it for you.'

With far less reluctance than she should have

been feeling Darcy undid the tie on her robe and it fell open, exposing her upper body. Max smiled, and it was wicked. His eyes had turned dark and golden.

Darcy felt so hot she feared bursting into flames there and then. It was hard to breathe.

Very slowly and deliberately he tipped the glass over her, until a small stream of icy water trickled down over her chest and breasts. She gasped and tensed, and was almost surprised when the water didn't hiss on contact with her hot skin.

Her nipples pebbled into tight peaks under Max's torturously slow administration, and when she was thoroughly drenched, with water running down over her belly and between her legs to where she was hottest of all, he put down the glass and pushed her robe back further, baring her completely.

He braced himself with his hands either side of her body, holding the robe back, keeping her captive. His gaze devoured her and he bent and dipped his head, his hot tongue a startling contrast to the cold water on her skin as he teased and tormented her breasts, tasting them and sucking each hard tip into his mouth until Darcy cried out and begged him to stop.

He lifted his head and smiled the smile of a master sorceror. 'We haven't even started, *dolcezza*… Lie back on the table.'

Unable to stay upright anyway, Darcy sank back and felt Max's big body push her legs wide, coming between them, baring her to him utterly.

He pressed kisses down her body, over the soft swell of her belly, and his big hands kept her open to him as his mouth descended between her legs and he found the scorching centre of her being. He stroked and licked her with sinful precision, until her hands were clasped in his hair and she was bucking uncontrollably into his mouth…

Later, when they'd made it back to the bedroom, they made love again. And again.

Darcy lifted her head from Max's chest and asked sleepily, 'So, will you tell me now?'

Max huffed a small chuckle. 'I should have known you wouldn't forget.'

Darcy rested her chin on her hand and said, 'Well…?'

Max shifted then, and she could tell he was mildly uncomfortable. But he said, 'I had arranged to take you to Venice… We were going to do a gondola ride and stay the night in a hotel on the Grand Canal.'

He lifted his head then, and looked at her with an endearingly rueful expression—very *un*Max-like.

'It would have been the worst kind of cliché, wouldn't it?'

Darcy's heart twisted painfully. 'Yes,' she whispered, 'but it would have been lovely.'

And then she ducked her head and feigned falling asleep, because she was terrified to admit to herself just how completely Max had seduced her.

CHAPTER NINE

THE FOLLOWING MORNING Darcy woke to an insistent prodding that was becoming more and more intimate as a hand smoothed down over her bare backside and squeezed firmly. She smiled and wriggled, hoping to entice the hand into further exploration, but instead it delivered a short, sharp *thwack*.

She raised her head from the pillow, blinking in the daylight. *Max*. Looking thoroughly gorgeous and disreputable with a growth of stubble. And he was dressed.

'What was that for?'

His hand smoothed where he'd slapped her so playfully. 'That was to get you up and out of bed… I want to take you out on the lake.'

At the word *lake* Darcy went very still. That big body of water that she'd avoided looking at—probably the only person on the planet who didn't enjoy the splendour of Lake Como.

She flipped over and held the sheet to her breasts. Max was already leaning back, tugging it out of her hand, but she held on with a death grip and tried to say, as breezily as possible, 'I'm quite tired, actually… Why don't you go? You can tell me how it was when you get back.'

Max stopped and his gaze narrowed on her. *Damn.*

'Why don't you want to go on the lake, Darcy? I've noticed that you barely look at it.'

She avoided his eye and sat up, feeling at a disadvantage lying down, and plucked at the sheet. 'I have issues with water. I can't swim.'

Carefully, Max said, 'You know, some fishermen can't swim—because they believe that if the sea claims them it's meant to be. It doesn't stop them going out on the water.'

Sensing that Max had no intention of going anywhere until she explained herself, she sighed deeply and said, 'I nearly drowned as a child. We had a pool at our house and my father was teaching me how to swim. My mother appeared and they started having a row. He got out to argue with her, forgetting about me… I don't know what happened… One minute I was okay and the next I couldn't feel the bottom any more and I'd started to drop like a stone. I must have drifted from the shallow end. They were so busy arguing, and I couldn't get their attention. All I could see was their arms gesticulating and then everything went black, there was a pain in my chest—'

Darcy hadn't even realised that she was bordering on hyperventilation until Max put a hand over hers, his fingers twining around hers to make her loosen her grip on the sheet.

'Darcy, it's okay—just breathe...'

She took a deep breath and looked at Max. 'That's why I don't want to go on the lake.'

He looked as if he was considering something, and then he said, 'Do you trust me?'

'Of course not,' she said facetiously.

Max rolled his eyes. 'I mean, would you trust me not to let any harm come to you?'

Physically...yes. Emotionally...no.

Damn. Darcy realised it as the heavy weight of inevitability hit her. She was falling for him. She was a disgrace to womankind. One hot air balloon ride and even hotter sex and she was—

'Okay?'

She blinked at Max, not having heard a word he'd said over the revelation banging around in her head like a warning klaxon going off after the fire had started and the horse had bolted.

'What?'

He said, with extreme patience, 'I want to take you somewhere and I promise you won't have to do anything you don't want to—okay?'

Right now even a lake was preferable to sitting alone with this new knowledge. 'Okay…'

And that was how she found herself, a few hours later, in a swimsuit, shivering with fear by the side of a kiddies' pool at a local adventure centre that Max said was owned by Dante D'Aquanni. A child ran past her and cannonballed into the pool.

Max was standing waist-deep in the water and saying, 'Look, I promise you'll be able to touch the bottom. Come on.'

Not even his body was helping to distract her right now.

'Sit on the edge and come in bit by bit.'

More because she didn't want to look like a total fool in front of Max than anything else, she gingerly sat down on the edge and put her legs in the water. Immediately she started shaking, re-membering how the water had sucked her down.

But Max had his hands on her waist and she gripped his arms.

Slowly, and with far more patience than she would have ever credited him with having, Max gently coaxed Darcy until she was standing in the water. Once she knew she could touch the bottom, he persuaded her to let him pull her along while she kicked her legs.

At one point she saw Max send a glower in the direction of some sniggering kids, but she didn't care.

And then he turned her on her back, which she only agreed to because he kept his arms underneath her. He was talking to her, telling her something, instructing her to kick her feet, and she was just getting comfortable with the feeling of floating when he said, 'Darcy?'

'Hmm?' It was nice, floating like this.

'Look.'

She lifted her head and saw Max with his hands in the air. It took a second for the fact that she was floating unaided to compute, and when it did she started to sink. But just as her head was about to go under she was caught, standing with her feet firmly on the bottom and Max holding her.

She was breathing rapidly and he was making soothing noises.

'I can't…can't be—believe you just let me go.'

'You were totally fine—you'll be swimming in no time.'

Darcy looked up at Max and her heart turned over. The pool was empty now, and she moved closer to him until their bodies were touching.

'I know one way of taking my mind off things…'

She reached up and wrapped her arms around Max's neck, moaning her satisfaction when his mouth came down on hers. Then he was lifting her, and she was wrapping her legs around his waist as he sat her down on the side of the pool and proceeded to do very adult things—until the discreet coughing of a staff member forced them apart like guilty teenagers.

Much later that night, after Darcy had shown Max her gratitude for helping her to start over-coming her fear of water in a very imaginative way, using her mouth to drive him over the edge of his control, Max couldn't sleep.

His body was still humming with pleasure… but not yet with the full sense of satisfaction that he usually felt after he'd bedded a woman. The sense of satisfaction that led to a feeling of restlessness and usually preceded his moving on.

Okay, so he knew he couldn't move on because he and Darcy were married—whether for real or not, they'd gone way over the boundaries of pretence now. But was that it? *No.* He'd be feeling this way if he and Darcy had started an affair anyway…and that revelation was disturbing.

No woman kept a hold over Max beyond the initial conquest. If he continued a liaison it was usually because it served some purpose not remotely romantic.

But things had escalated with Darcy so fast that his head felt as if it was spinning. She'd made him work for it, but it hadn't really been game-playing. And the final capitulation… It hadn't been sweet—it had been fast and furious and intense.

Even now he knew that if she was to turn to him he'd be ready to take her again and again. And tomorrow all over again.

He cursed softly and got out of bed and went

downstairs, raiding Dante's drinks cabinet for some of his fine whisky. He went out to the terrace, where the sound of the lake lapping against the shore should have been calming, but instead Max was remembering the look of stark terror on Darcy's face as he'd had to coax her into the pool.

Inferno. Since when did he mess about in paddling pools, teaching someone to swim? Yet he couldn't deny the sheer pleasure he'd taken from seeing her face lose its dread in the pool.

It had given him a kind of satisfaction that he usually reserved for each pinnacle he conquered on his way to the ultimate acceptance and respect in business. Which he still hadn't attained.

A shiver of something cold crawled up Max's spine—a memory...crying, feeling as though his guts were going to fall out of his body, his legs shaking...his mother gripping him. *'Stop snivelling. I'm taking you with me.'*

He'd told Darcy practically everything. More than he'd ever told anyone else.

He went even colder and realised that he wasn't even sure he recognised himself any more. Who *was* this person who made impromptu wedding proposals? Who chased a woman around a kitchen with a glass of water?

The memory made Max cringe now.

He'd let emotion get in the way once before and had paid the price.

Another more pertinent memory came back: the day he'd seen his old nemesis while he'd been foraging in that bin in Paris. It was one of those moments in life when the fates had literally laughed in his face just to torture him.

One of them had come back and handed Max a five-euro note. Max had taken it and ripped it up, before letting it drop to the ground and spitting on it.

He hadn't needed anyone then, and he didn't need anyone now. He knew better than anybody how life could be as fickle and as random as a pair of dice rolling to a stop, dictating the future.

But he'd changed that. The power to dictate everything lay with *him*.

He'd fought for this control over his destiny and he was damned if he was going to let it slip out of his grasp now just because he was forgetting where his priorities lay. Anger licked through his blood at the knowledge of just how far off course he was in danger of straying.

Darcy was distracting him.

And he was fogetting the most important thing: *She was just a means to an end.*

The following morning, on the plane ride home, Darcy didn't need to be psychic to know that something had changed during the night. Max was back in ruthless boss mode. Brusque. Abrupt.

He'd already been up when she'd woken, dressed and packed.

She'd felt flustered. 'You should have woken me.'

He'd been cool. 'I have some work to catch up on in Dante's study. We'll leave in half an hour.'

She couldn't fault Max for wanting to jump straight back into things—after all Montgomery's party was right around the corner, sealing the deal... But it was almost as if he had just carved out these few days to seduce Darcy and now it was mission accomplished and he was moving on.

She'd expected this. But she hadn't expected it to be quite so brutally obvious.

Was it a dream or had this man gripped her hips so hard last night that she still bore the marks of his fingers on her flesh? Had she imagined that he'd held her ruthlessly still so that he could thrust up into her body over and over again, until she'd been begging for mercy, and only then finally tipped them both over the edge?

No, because she'd seen the marks in the mirror in the bathroom and her muscles still ached pleasurably.

Darcy felt a little shattered—as if the pieces that Max had rent asunder deep inside her would never come back together again.

Maybe he was regretting the weekend…realising that it had all been a huge mistake. Realising that she hadn't been worth all that effort… the shopping, the hot air balloon… But even if he was, she wasn't going to regret it. She'd made her choice.

'Darcy?'

She looked at Max, who was frowning impatiently. 'I need you to take some notes—we'll be going straight to the office from the airport.'

Ignoring the voices screaming at her to leave

it alone, Darcy turned to him and said, 'So that's it, then? Honeymoon over. Back to work.'

Max looked at her and she shivered.

'What did you expect?'

'All that seduction…the hot air balloon…'

Max shrugged. 'You knew I wanted you in my bed—whatever it took.'

Incredible pain lanced her. 'I see.'

For a moment Darcy thought she might be sick, but she forced it down. She had to get away from Max. She hated it that she wasn't strong enough to weather the evidence of his ruthlessness in front of him.

She unbuckled her belt quickly and stood up, muttering something about the bathroom. Once locked inside the small space she saw her face in the mirror, leached of colour.

Stupid, stupid Darcy. How could she have forgotten that this man's two main traits were being ruthless and being more ruthless. He must have been laughing himself silly when Darcy had all but begged him to go to bed after his *piéce de résistance*: the balloon ride. It would be tainted in her head for ever now.

She thought of the pool then, of Max's patience

and gentle coaxing, and this time she couldn't stop the contents of her stomach from lurching up.

When she'd composed herself she looked at herself in the mirror again. She had to get a grip. She'd lost herself for a moment and she'd done it willingly—her hands held tightly onto the sink—but it had only been for a moment. A weekend. She was okay. She could put this momentary weakness behind her and get on with things, and as soon as the ink was dry on the deal with Montgomery she'd be gone.

When they returned to Max's apartment after going into the office Max disappeared into his study to do some more work. Darcy took herself out for a long walk around the centre of Rome, coming back with no sense of peace in her head or her heart.

She was feeling increasingly angry with herself for giving in to his smooth seduction, having known what it was likely to do to her.

He was still working when she returned, so she ate alone and went to bed, telling herself that the ache she felt was just her pathetic imagination.

After midnight, just when she was hovering on the edge of sleep, Max came into her room.

'This isn't my room.'

Darcy came up on one elbow, anger rising. 'No, it's *my* room.'

'So why aren't you in my bed?'

'Because,' Darcy said tersely, well and truly awake now, 'I don't care for the hot and cold routine, and you've made it perfectly clear that now we've consummated the relationship you're done with any niceties.'

Max came close to the bed and Darcy hated the way her blood sizzled with anticipation.

'I never said I was *nice*, Darcy,' he pointed out. 'Are you going to come to my bed?'

'No,' Darcy said mutinously.

Max just shrugged and left, and Darcy let out a shaky sigh of…*disappointment*. She lambasted herself. She was pathetic. And then her mouth dropped open when Max walked back in with a bunch of clothes and some toiletries.

She watched, dumbfounded, as he proceeded to strip and get into the bed beside her. He leaned on one elbow, unselfconsciously naked in the way that only the most gorgeous people could be, and those tawny eyes glinted with pure devilment.

'The honeymoon is over, but this isn't.'

He reached for her and Darcy had a split second to realise that she could take the moral high ground and resist Max's arrogant pull or, as she asked herself belligerently, why shouldn't she use Max as he was using her? Take her own pleasure from him until *she* was sated?

That was the weak logic she used, anyway, as she hurled herself back into the fire.

When she woke in the morning and all those little voices were ready to rip her to shreds for her weakness she resolutely ignored them and told herself she could do this. Max didn't have the monopoly on being cold and ruthless.

As the days progressed, getting closer to the time they'd be leaving for Scotland, their working hours got longer. And in the nights…the passion between them seemed to burn brighter and fiercer with each coupling. Darcy's anger with herself and Max added something that seemed to hurl her over the edge further and further each time, until she was left spent and shaking.

Some nights Max seemed to forget what part he was playing, and he'd scoop her close and hold her to him with arms like vises around her. It was on those nights that Darcy knew she was fooling herself the most.

This game she was playing with Max *was* costing her. She knew that she wasn't strong enough emotionally to keep it up indefinitely, and that it would have to stop before she got burned in the fire completely.

But just not right now…

The Montgomery estate, north of Inverness

Darcy huffed out a breath and stopped to look at the view. It was spectacular, and it soothed some of the tension inside her. Hills and mountains stretched as far as the eye could see, and small lochs were dotted here and there like black pools. Clouds scudded across the blue sky.

In true Scottish fashion, even though it was summer, it had rained since they'd arrived, a couple of days ago. But now the sun was out and the countryside sparkled.

Darcy was relishing a rare chance to be alone. She'd had enough of Max's tense mood infecting her own.

Wily old Montgomery was playing hard to get right to the end. The party was tonight, and Max still wasn't sure where he stood. To make things even worse, there were several other high-profile financiers invited. Darcy almost felt sorry for Max—but then she thought of the sensual torture he'd put her through the previous night and promptly felt *un*sorry for him.

She sat down on a piece of soft springy ground and sighed, pushing her hair back off her hot cheeks. Here against this timeless and peaceful backdrop she couldn't keep running from her own conscience and her heart.

In spite of everything, she'd fallen for Max. Self-disgust that she should fall for someone so ruthless and single-minded took the edge off the awful tendency she felt to cry. And yet her bruised heart still pathetically wanted to believe that the Max she'd seen that weekend in Como was real…

One thing Darcy *did* know was that Max fooled himself as much as everyone around him. He had feelings, all right, but they were so buried after years of hiding them that it would be like mining for diamonds trying to extract them.

She knew why her instinct had always warned her off deeper commitment if this was the pain it brought.

But she couldn't continue with the status quo. It was a form of self-destruction that Darcy knew she had to stop now—he'd worn her down and broken her apart like the pro he was, and she couldn't let it continue.

Max wasn't going to like it, but he'd get over it. He'd have to, because nothing would compel her to change her mind. Not even his singular seduction.

That night Darcy felt jittery, and Max said beside her, 'Stop fidgeting.'

She sent him a dark look. She had her arm tucked into his, for all the world the happy newly married couple.

Mrs Montgomery had come up to Darcy earlier and said confidentially, 'Why, he's a new man, my dear. He was always so *brooding* before.'

Darcy had smiled weakly and looked to see Max

throwing his head back and laughing at something his companion said. Her gut had twisted. *Was* he different? And then she'd clamped down on that very dangerous line of thought.

She was wearing the royal blue satin dress she'd seen in the window of the boutique that day in Milan. When she'd spotted it hanging in her wardrobe in Max's apartment it had given her a jolt as she'd recalled a much more light-hearted Max.

She hadn't wanted to wear it, but he'd insisted. And the look in his eyes when she'd put it on had been nearly enough to make her skin sizzle.

He'd growled, 'If we weren't already late for dinner I'd lock the door to this room, make you take it off, make love to you and then make you put it on again… But I'd probably only want to take it off again…'

A voice had wheedled in Darcy's head—*What's one more night…?*—and she'd shut it out. She couldn't afford one more night with Max.

The crowd was making a toast now, to Cecil Montgomery, his smiling wife and their four children and assorted grandchildren. Darcy's heart constricted. Happiness was there for some people. The very few.

She felt Max tense beside her. Time for the announcement.

Montgomery started by going into a long-winded account of his career, clearly building up to the big moment. Darcy bit her lip and looked at Max, but his face was expressionless.

'As many of you will know, it's been my life's work to cultivate, protect and grow the famous private equity fund of this family that goes back generations. It's my legacy to my children and grandchildren—not to mention our very important philanthropic work...'

Montgomery cleared his throat and kept going.

'As we all know in these uncertain times, expert advice is necessary to ensure the growth and protection of anything of importance. And this fund is not just my life's work, but my ancestors'. It's been of the utmost importance that I choose someone who has those sensibilities in mind. Who understands the importance of family and legacy...for the benefit of not only my own family but also much larger concerns.'

He paused dramatically and then took a breath.

'There is only one person I would trust with this great responsibility, and I'm pleased to announce that that man is...Maximiliano Fonseca Roselli.'

Darcy could feel the surge of emotion in Max's body. He shook with it. She waited for him to turn and acknowledge her, as much for appearances' sake as anything else, but after a moment he just disengaged her arm from his and strode forward to accept Montgomery's handshake and congratulations.

Darcy could see people looking at her. It was as brutal a sign of where she really stood in his life as a slap in the face, and she realised then that all along she'd been harbouring some kind of pathetic hope that perhaps she was mistaken and he *did* feel *something* for her.

Seeing the crowd lining up to congratulate Max, Darcy took advantage of the moment to slip out of the room and walk blindly through the castle, eyes blurred but refusing to let the tears well and fall.

She would not cry over this man. She would *not*.

* * *

Max cursed silently. Where *was* she? He knew Darcy was petite, but he'd realised that somehow he had an uncanny knack of finding her glossy dark brown head in any crowd. He thought of her as she'd stood before him in the bedroom not long ago, the deep blue of the satin dress curving around her body in such a way that it had made him feel animalistic. He'd almost forgotten what the evening was about. *Almost.*

Lingering tendrils of relief and triumph had snaked through him as he'd forged his way through the throng, accepting congratulations and slaps on the back. Funny, he'd expected to bask in this moment for a lot longer, but he was distracted.

Darcy. Where was she?

She'd been standing beside him when Montgomery had called out his name and his first instinct had been to turn to her. She'd done this with him. He wouldn't have done it without her. *He'd wanted to share it with her.*

The surge of alien emotion that had gripped him had caught him right in his throat and at the back of his eyes, making them sting. Horror-struck, in a nano-second he'd been aware that he was on the verge of tears and about to let Darcy see it. So at the last second he'd pulled away and strode forward. Not wanting her to see the rawness he was feeling. Not ready for the scrutiny of those huge blue eyes that saw too much.

He cursed again. She wasn't here. A quick tour of the surrounding rooms didn't reveal her either, and Max made his way to the bedroom with a growing sense of unease.

When he opened the door to the bedroom the sense of unease coalesced into a black mass in his gut. Darcy barely looked up when he walked in. She'd changed into black trousers and a stripy top. Her hair was pulled back into a ponytail. She looked about sixteen. She was packing her suitcase.

Max folded his arms, as if that might ease the constriction in his chest.

'What are you doing?'

She glanced at him, her face expressionless. 'I'm leaving.'

Seizing on his default mechanism of acerbity, Max drawled, 'I think I could have deduced that much.'

Darcy shrugged as she pulled the top of the suitcase down and started to zip it up. 'Well, then, if it's that obvious why ask?'

Anger started to flicker to life in Max's gut as the full impact of what he was looking at sank in. *She was leaving.* He didn't like the clutch of panic. Panic was not something he ever felt.

'What's going on, Darcy? They've only just made the announcement—dinner hasn't even been served yet.'

Darcy stopped zipping up the bag and looked at him. For a moment he saw something flicker in her eyes but then it was gone.

'I'm done, Max. I've more than paid my dues as your convenient wife. When you can't even acknowledge me in your moment of glory it's pretty obvious that I've become superfluous to your requirements.'

The panic gripped him tighter. He'd messed up. 'Look, Darcy, I know I couldn't have achieved this without you—'

She laughed, short and sharp. 'You had this all along. I think Montgomery just enjoyed watching you jump through hoops... It's not many deals or many men Maximiliano Fonseca Roselli will do that for.'

Darcy picked up the jacket that was laid over the back of a nearby chair and shrugged it on, turning those huge blue eyes on him.

'What did you expect to happen now, Max? Some kind of fake domestic idyll? The deal is done. This is over. There's no more need for the charade.'

Max felt tight all over, in the grip of something dark and hot. He bit out, 'You won't even stay one more night.' He didn't pose it as a question, already hating himself for saying it.

Darcy shook her head and her glossy pony-tail slid over one shoulder. 'No. I've given you enough of my time, Max. More than enough.'

Was it his imagination or had there been a catch in her voice? Max couldn't hear through the dull roaring in his head. He felt himself tee-tering on the edge of something... Asking her to stay? But, as she'd said, for what? What did he want from her now? And what was this terri-fying swooping of emotion, threatening to push him over the edge, spurred on by the panic which made his insides feel as loose as they'd felt tight a moment ago…?

He'd only ever felt like this once before. When he'd stood before another woman—his mother—and let her see the full extent of his vulnerability and pain. He'd tipped over the edge then and his life had never been the same.

He was not going to tip over the edge for anyone else. He had just achieved the pinnacle of his success. What did he need Darcy for? He had everything that he'd ever wanted. He could go on from here and live his life and know that he was untouchable, that he had surpassed every one of his naysayers and doubters. Every one of the bullies.

He and Luca would finally be equals—on his terms.

The realisation that no great sense of satisfaction accompanied that knowledge was not something Max wanted to dwell on. Suddenly he was quite eager to get on with things. Without that incisive bluer than blue gaze tracking his every movement.

The fact that he looked at Darcy even now and felt nothing but hunger was irritating, but he told himself that once she was out of his orbit it would die down…fade away.

He would take a new lover. Start again.

He uncrossed his arms. 'Your bonus will be in your bank by Monday. My solicitor will work out the details of the divorce.'

'Thank you.' Darcy avoided his eye now, picking up her bag.

A knock came to the door and she looked up. 'That'll be the taxi. The housekeeper is sending someone up for my bags when it arrives.'

Max had pushed everything he was feeling down so deep that he was slightly light-headed. Like a robot, he moved over to the bed and took Darcy's suitcase easily in one hand. He took it to the door and opened it, handing it out to the young man on the other side. One of the estate staff.

And then Darcy was in the doorway, close enough for him to smell her scent. It had an immediate effect on him, making his body hard.

Damn her. Right now he was more than ready to see the back of her. That edge was beckoning again, panic flaring.

He stepped back, allowing her to leave the

room. He forced himself to be solicitous even as he had a sudden urge to haul her back into the room and slam the door shut, locking them both inside.

And what then? asked a snide voice.

Another one answered: *Chaos*.

'Good luck, Darcy. If you need anything get in touch.'

'I won't.' Her voice was definitely husky now, and she wasn't looking at him. 'But thank you. Goodbye, Max.'

CHAPTER TEN

DARCY WASN'T SURE how she managed it, but she stayed in a state of calm numbness until she was on the train at Inverness Station and it was pulling out in the direction of Edinburgh, followed by London.

As the train picked up speed, though, it was as if its motion was peeling her skin back to expose where her heart lay in tatters, just under her breastbone. It had taken almost every ounce of her strength to stand before Max and maintain that icy, unconcerned front.

She just made it to the toilet in time, where she sat on the closed lid, shuddering and weeping and swaying as the train took her further and further away from the man who had taken all her vulnerabilities and laid them bare for his own ends.

And she couldn't even blame him. She'd handed herself over to his ruthless heartlessness lock, stock and barrel. *She'd* made that choice.

Three months later

Darcy climbed up the steps from the tube and emerged in a quiet road of a leafy suburb in north London. Well, not so leafy now that autumn was here in force, stripping everything bare.

After walking for a few minutes she hitched her bags to one hand as she dug out her key and put it in the front door of her apartment building. A familiar dart of pleasure rushed through her. *Her apartment building.* Which housed her bijou ground-floor two-bedroomed apartment that had French doors leading out to her own private back garden.

The bonus Max had provided had more than covered the cost of the apartment with cash—making the sale fast and efficient. She'd moved in three weeks ago.

Max. He was always on the periphery of her mind, but Darcy shied away from looking at him too directly—like avoiding the glare of the sun for fear of going blind.

For a month after she'd left him in Scotland she'd had to endure seeing him emblazoned over every paper and magazine: the wunderkind of the financial world, accepted into the highest eche-lons where heads of state and the most powerful people in the world hailed his genius.

The emotion she'd felt thinking that he finally must have found some peace had mocked her.

There'd been pictures of him in gossip columns too, attending glittering events with a different beautiful woman on his arm each time. The pain Darcy had felt had been like a hot dagger skew-ering her belly, so she'd stopped watching the news or reading the papers.

She put her shopping away with little enthusi-asm and thought idly of inviting her neighbour from upstairs for something to eat. John was the first person to make her laugh since she'd left Max.

After a quick trip upstairs, and John's totally overjoyed acceptance of her invitation—*'Sweetie, you are the best! I was about to die of hunger... like literally die!'*—Darcy went back downstairs and prepared some dinner, feeling marginally better.

She could get through this and emerge intact. *She could*, she vowed as she skewered some chicken with a little more force than necessary.

* * *

'You know, if you ever want to tell Uncle John about the bastard who done you wrong, I'll get a few boxes of wine and we'll hunker down for the weekend. Make a pity party of it.'

Darcy smiled as she picked up the plates and said wryly, as she hid the dart of inevitable pain, 'Is it that obvious?'

John took a sip of wine, his eyes following Darcy as she went into the kitchen. 'Hate to say it, love, but *yes*. You've got that unmistakable Eeyore droop to your lovely mouth and eyes.'

Darcy laughed just as a knock came to her door. She looked at John and he shrugged. 'Must be another neighbour?'

She went over to open it and swung it wide to reveal a very tall, very beautifully disheveled man with dark blond hair, olive skin and tawny eyes. And a distinctive scar. Dressed all in black.

She could almost hear John's jaw drop behind her. And she was belatedly and bizarrely aware that she was still smiling after his comment.

The smile slid off her face as shock and disbelief set in. 'Max.'

'Darcy.'

Her name on his tongue curled through her like warm honey, oozing over the ice packed around her heart.

'Can I come in?'

It was shock that made her act like an automaton, standing back, opening the door wider so that Max could step in, bringing with him the cool tang of autumn.

Darcy saw him clock John and the way his face tightened and darkened. His jaw was shadowed with stubble, adding to his general air of effortless disrepute.

'I'm interrupting?' He sounded stiff. Not at all like his usual insouciant self. Fazed by nothing.

Darcy tore her eyes off Max, almost afraid that he might disappear, to see that John had somehow picked his jaw back up off the ground and was standing up.

'No, I was just leaving.'

She was glad he'd spoken, because she wasn't sure she could speak.

She felt a quick supportive squeeze of her hand and then her neighbour was gone, closing the door behind him.

Darcy realised how close she was standing to

Max and how huge he seemed in her small flat. Had he always been so huge?

She moved away, towards the table that still held the dinner detritus.

'You've lost weight.' Max's tone was almost accusing.

Darcy turned around. Of all the things she'd expected to hear from him it hadn't been that. And for someone who'd spent much of her lifetime lamenting her fuller figure it was ironic that in the past few months she'd managed to drop the guts of a stone without even trying.

She crossed her arms, suddenly angry that Max was here. Invading her space. Invading her mind. Being angry with him was easier than analysing other, far more dangerous emotions.

'You've hardly come all this way to comment on my weight, Max.' Her insides tightened. 'Is it something to do with the divorce?' She hadn't received the papers yet, but had been expecting something soon.

Max shook his head and ran a hand through his hair, mussing it up. The gesture was so familiar that Darcy had to bite her lip for fear of emitting some sound.

'No, it's not about the divorce…it's something else.' Max started to prowl around the flat, as if inspecting it, looking into the kitchen. He turned to face her, frowning. 'Why didn't you buy a bigger place?'

Darcy felt defensive. 'I didn't want a mortgage and I like this—it suits me.'

'I would have given you more money for somewhere bigger.'

She dropped her arms, hands spread out. 'Max…why are you here?'

He looked at her so intently that she began to sweat, becoming self-conscious in her roll-neck top and jeans. It had been 'Casual Friday' at her new job that day. Working as PA to the CEO of a dynamic software company was sufficiently new and different to give her the illusion that she could avoid thinking about Max during the day. That illusion was now well and truly shattered.

'I wanted to make sure you had your place… that you were settled. I owe you that.'

Darcy's insides fluttered. 'I have it, Max. And I wouldn't have had it without you.'

He looked at her. 'You also wouldn't have had

the media speculation and the intense scrutiny afforded to our marriage.'

Darcy almost winced. After she'd left him the papers had been consumed by what had happened to her. Luckily she'd been able to return to London and disappear into the crowds, unassuming enough that no one recognised her. They'd been married for such a short amount of time it had really only registered as a story in Italy.

'At least it didn't affect your deal with Montgomery.'

Max's mouth tightened. 'Your assessment of him was right. He'd always intended giving me the fund—he just enjoyed making me work for it.'

Darcy sat down heavily onto the chair behind her. 'So we never had to go through with the wedding?'

Max shook his head.

He came forward and touched the back of the chair next to hers and said, 'Do you mind if I sit?'

Darcy waved a hand vaguely, barely aware of Max's uncharacteristic reticence or solicitude. Or the starkness of his features.

'The man who was just here…he is your boy-friend?'

Darcy came back into the room from imagining what might have happened, or *not* happened, if they hadn't married. She didn't like to admit that she preferred the version where they'd married. In spite of the pain.

Not really thinking, she said, 'No, John's my neighbour. And he's gay.'

Max sucked in a breath and Darcy looked at him sharply. He looked gaunt. The flutters got stronger and she hated it.

Sharply, she said, 'Not that it's any business of yours. You've hardly been wasting any time proving that our marriage was a farce. I've seen those pictures of you with women.'

Max stood up then and shrugged off his jacket, revealing a long-sleeved top that clung almost indecently to his hard torso. For a second Darcy didn't hear what he was saying…she was too hot and distracted.

'…doing everything I could to try and pretend things can go back to normal.'

Darcy blinked. Max was pacing, talking as if to himself. She swivelled in the chair so she could watch him. He was like a glorious caged lion in the confines of her flat.

He turned to her. 'The evening Montgomery announced that he was giving me the fund to manage I was so overcome with emotion that I couldn't bear for you to see it. In case you'd see that the front I'd put up after Como was just that: a stupid, pathetic front to hide behind.'

'Max, what are you talking about?'

But he wasn't listening to her. He was pacing again, becoming increasingly angry. At himself.

'When I went upstairs and saw you packing I felt panic. *Panic!* I've never panicked in my life—not even when I realised I had no option but to live on the streets.'

Darcy stood up, but Max continued.

'And then you were standing there, so cool and collected, asking me what else I wanted now that I had achieved my goal.'

Max stopped and turned to face her again.

'You were asking me to step out into an abyss and I was too much of a coward to do it. I told myself that I had everything I needed, that I didn't need you. I told myself that the hunger I felt every time I looked at you, which got worse if I wasn't near you, would fade in time. So I let you go, and I went back down to that function, and I told people you'd had to leave for a family emergency. I told myself I was *fine*. That I would be *fine*.'

He shook his head.

'But I wasn't. I'm not. The day my parents split my brother and I up I showed my emotions. I cried because I wanted to stay with my mother.'

His mouth twisted.

'I couldn't believe that she was going to leave me behind with my father… I had no thought for my brother, only myself. But he was the stoic one. I was the one falling apart. And so she took me, and I spent my life paying for it. When you were leaving me I wanted to slam the door shut and lock it to prevent you going. I didn't. Because I was afraid of what might happen if I just let all that emotion out. I was afraid my world would turn on its axis again and I'd lose it all just when I'd finally got it. I was afraid I'd lose myself again.'

Darcy's breathing was erratic. 'What are you saying, Max?'

'I wanted you to be settled, to find the home

you wanted so badly. I wanted you to know that you have a choice.'

'A choice for what?'

Max took a deep breath. 'I want you to come back to me. I want you to stay being my wife. But if you don't want that I'll leave you alone.'

Darcy shook her head as if trying to clear it. 'You want me back…because it's convenient? Because—?'

Max held up a hand. *'No.'* And then he sliced into the heart of her with all the precision of a master surgeon. 'I want you to come back because you've broken me in two. I finally have everything I've always wanted—everything I've always *thought* I wanted. But it means nothing any more because you're not with me. I love you, Darcy.'

Darcy blinked. *I love you?* This was a Max she'd never seen before. Humbled. Broken. *Real.* For a second she couldn't believe it, but the depth of pain in his eyes scored at her own heart—because she knew what it felt like.

She whispered through the lump in her throat. 'There's never been a choice, Max. Not since the day we met again.' She waved a hand, indicating the flat. 'I finally have everything I thought I wanted too—a home of my own, a base—but it's meaningless because *you're* my centre.'

Max's face leached of colour. 'What are you saying?'

Darcy's vision blurred with tears and she could feel her heart knitting back together. 'I'm saying I love you too, you big idiot.'

She wasn't sure who moved, but suddenly she was in his arms with hers wrapped around him so tightly she could hardly breathe. They staggered back until Max fell onto the couch, taking Darcy with him so she was sitting on his lap.

She wasn't even aware she was crying until she felt Max's hand moving up and down her back rhythmically, heard him soothing her with words in Italian...*dolcezza mia...amore...*

Darcy finally lifted her head and looked up at Max, who smoothed some hair off her forehead. She manoeuvred herself so that she was straddling his lap and both her hands were on his shoulders. She saw the way his eyes flared and colour came back into his cheeks and moved experimentally, exulting when she could feel the evidence of his arousal.

She moved her hips against him subtly, but pulled back when he tried to kiss her. 'Who were the women?'

His eyes flashed with a hint of the old Max. 'They were my attempt to be *normal* again. And none of them was *you*. Which was *very* annoying.'

He attempted to kiss her again but Darcy arched away, making Max scowl.

'Did you kiss any of them?'

Max's scowl deepened. 'I tried.'

Darcy went still as a hot skewer of jealousy ripped through her.

'But I couldn't do it. For one thing they were too tall, too skinny, too chatty about stupid things. *Not you*.'

Darcy smiled. 'Good.'

'What about Jack, are you sure he's gay?'

Now Max looked as if he wanted to skewer someone with a hot poker.

Darcy rolled her eyes. 'It's *John*. And yes, he's gay, Max. I can practically hear him drooling from here.'

Max looked smug. 'Good.'

Darcy brought her hands up to Max's face, cupping it. And then she bent her head to kiss her husband, showing him with everything in her just how much she loved him. The emotion was almost painful. Max's hands moved all over her, undoing her hair, lifting her top up and off so that she was just in her bra.

She rested her forehead against his, wondering if this was a dream. 'I thought I'd never see you again.'

Max's hands closed tight around her hips. He shook his head. 'I would have come sooner, but I was a coward, and then when I heard you'd bought a place already I thought you were moving on.'

Darcy's heart clenched. She looked into Max's eyes. 'You're not a coward, Max...anything but.'

She ran a finger lightly down over his scar and he caught her hand and pressed a kiss to the centre of her palm. He looked at her. 'The night we met Montgomery for dinner...?'

Darcy nodded.

'I think that on some subconscious level I knew I wanted you badly enough to tie you to me by any means necessary. The thing is, I wouldn't have made that impetuous decision if you had been anyone else… It's because it was *you*, and I had to have you no matter what.'

Max's confession eased some tiny last piece of doubt inside Darcy. She smiled and shifted against him again, putting her hands on the couch behind him, pushing her breasts wantonly towards Max's mouth.

'I think we've said all that needs to be said for now.'

Max smiled at her, long and slow and with a cocksure *Maxness* that told Darcy it wouldn't be long before he was back to his arrogant self again.

'I love you, Signora Fonseca Roselli. These last three months have been a torture I wouldn't wish on my worst enemy. You're never leaving my side again.'

She brought her hand around to the back of his head, gripping his hair, tugging at it. 'I love *you*, Signor Fonseca Roselli, and I have no intention of ever leaving your side again.'

And then she bent her head and pressed a kiss to the corner of his mouth.

Max growled his frustration, cupping her jaw

and angling her head so that within seconds they were kissing so deeply that there was no need for any more words for quite a while.

EPILOGUE

FOR TWO AND a half years Darcy and Max lived an idyllic existence, locked happily in a bubble of love and sensuality. She continued to work for him—but only when he travelled abroad and they didn't want to be separated.

Meanwhile, Darcy set up a business as a freelance business interpreter and frequently travelled all over Europe for different assignments—which Max invariably grumbled about. Darcy ignored him. He liked to use them as an excuse to surprise her, anyway—like the time he'd appeared in Paris when she'd walked out of a meeting and whisked her off on his private jet to the romantic and windswept west coast of Ireland. They'd ended up staying in Dromoland Castle for a week...

They bought a house in Rome's leafy exclusive Monteverde district and together made it a true home, keeping on her place in London as a piedà-terre. Max still hadn't taken the plunge and bought a football club, but he spent lots of time at matches, investigating various teams.

One of the things Darcy was happiest about, though, was the rebuilding of Max's relationship with his brother Luca. It had been slow at first, but with the help of Luca's wife Serena, whom Darcy now counted as a firm friend, the two men were now in regular contact and needed no encouragement to spend time together. Which suited Darcy and Serena fine, especially when *they* wanted to catch up, without their husbands doing that annoying attention-seeking thing they did.

Max's relationship with his mother stayed strained, but he'd finally come to terms with the way she was and, together with Darcy, had managed to learn how to support her without taking on her addictions as his responsibility.

As for Darcy with her parents, she had learnt to tolerate their various love catastrophes with much more humour and less of a feeling of impending doom.

And then, two and a half years into their marriage, Darcy had walked white-faced into their bedroom one morning, holding a small plastic stick.

Max had looked at her and immediately frowned, concerned. *'Ché cosa?'*

She'd felt a very ominous tightening of her chest at the thought of his reaction and what it might to do them. This was the one thing they'd never really talked about, and when Serena had fallen pregnant Darcy had seen how Max had reacted in private—by shutting it out. So she knew this was a potential minefield for him—for the young boy who had been so hurt by his own parents.

Silently she'd handed him the plastic and watched as comprehension dawned.

He'd gone a little green and looked at her. 'But...*how*?'

She'd shrugged, feeling slightly sick herself at his reaction. 'I don't know. I've never missed a pill... But I had that flu a while back...'

They'd never spoken about Darcy coming off the pill. She'd hoped with time that they would discuss it...but now it was beyond discussion. She was pregnant.

She'd watched Max absorb the news, much in the same way she was, but whereas *she* felt a tiny burgeoning excitement starting to grow, she feared Max might feel the opposite.

After a long moment he'd looked at her resolutely and had come to sit on the end of the bed, the sheets tangled around his naked body. He'd reached for her and pulled her down onto his lap.

Her heart had clenched to see the clear battle going on in the golden depths of those amazing eyes but she'd waited for him to speak, and eventually he'd said gruffly, 'You know that this was never going to be easy for me…but I love you… and I can't imagine not loving any baby of ours even if I am scared to death of hurting it as Luca and I were hurt…'

Overcome with emotion at the extent of his willingness not to run scared from this, which he might have done before, Darcy had felt tears prickle behind her eyes as she'd cupped Max's jaw and pressed her mouth to his, kissing him gently.

'I trust in you, Max. You who overcame adversity time and again and who survived your own parents' woeful lack of care. You aren't capable of giving anything less than one hundred per cent commitment and love to any baby of ours. They'll be the luckiest child in the world to have you as a father.'

He'd looked at her, his eyes suspiciously bright. 'And you as their mother. I wouldn't want to do this with anyone else.'

And now, eight months later the reality that they'd come to terms with was manifest *times two*!

Darcy opened tired but happy eyes to take in the scene in the corner of her private hospital room.

And she would have laughed if she hadn't been afraid of bursting her Caesarean stitches.

Max was sprawled in a chair, shirt open at the neck haphazardly, jeans low on his hips. His hair was even more mussed than usual, his jaw stubbled. If it hadn't been for the two small bundles carefully balanced, one in the crook of each arm, he might have looked like the reprobate playboy he'd used to be, coming home after a debauched night out.

But he was no playboy. He was a lover and a husband. And now a father. Of twins.

They'd realised that Darcy must have had twins somewhere in her family line too when they'd been informed of the news by their consultant early on in the pregnancy. Much to their stunned shock.

Max was looking at his son and daughter as if they were the most prized jewels in the world. Awed. Domino and Daisy—named after Max's Italian grandfather and Darcy's English grandmother. They'd asked the Montgomerys—who had become good friends—to be godparents to a baby each, and already the older couple had proved to be far more dedicated than *real* grandparents.

Max said now to his son, whose eyes were shut tight, 'Dom, just because you came first it doesn't mean anything. In fact...' He looked at his daughter, whose eyes were open wide, and said, *sotto voce*, 'We'll pretend *you* came first, Daisy, hmm? That way he won't be able to get too big for his boots...and your *mamma* has had a lot of drugs, so maybe we can convince her of this too...?'

He looked up at Darcy then, and smiled goofily at being caught out. Love made her chest swell so much she had to take a breath. She smiled back and love stretched between them, binding them all together for ever.

* * * * *

MILLS & BOON®
Large Print – October 2015

THE BRIDE FONSECA NEEDS
Abby Green

SHEIKH'S FORBIDDEN CONQUEST
Chantelle Shaw

PROTECTING THE DESERT HEIR
Caitlin Crews

SEDUCED INTO THE GREEK'S WORLD
Dani Collins

TEMPTED BY HER BILLIONAIRE BOSS
Jennifer Hayward

**MARRIED FOR THE
PRINCE'S CONVENIENCE**
Maya Blake

THE SICILIAN'S SURPRISE WIFE
Tara Pammi

HIS UNEXPECTED BABY BOMBSHELL
Soraya Lane

FALLING FOR THE BRIDESMAID
Sophie Pembroke

A MILLIONAIRE FOR CINDERELLA
Barbara Wallace

FROM PARADISE...TO PREGNANT!
Kandy Shepherd

0915 Rom LP

MILLS & BOON®
Large Print – November 2015

The Ruthless Greek's Return
Sharon Kendrick

Bound by the Billionaire's Baby
Cathy Williams

Married for Amari's Heir
Maisey Yates

A Taste of Sin
Maggie Cox

Sicilian's Shock Proposal
Carol Marinelli

Vows Made in Secret
Louise Fuller

The Sheikh's Wedding Contract
Andie Brock

A Bride for the Italian Boss
Susan Meier

The Millionaire's True Worth
Rebecca Winters

The Earl's Convenient Wife
Marion Lennox

Vettori's Damsel in Distress
Liz Fielding

MILLS & BOON®

Why shop at millsandboon.co.uk?

Each year, thousands of romance readers find their perfect read at millsandboon.co.uk. That's because we're passionate about bringing you the very best romantic fiction. Here are some of the advantages of shopping at www.millsandboon.co.uk:

* **Get new books first**—you'll be able to buy your favourite books one month before they hit the shops

* **Get exclusive discounts**—you'll also be able to buy our specially created monthly collections, with up to 50% off the RRP

* **Find your favourite authors**—latest news, interviews and new releases for all your favourite authors and series on our website, plus ideas for what to try next

* **Join in**—once you've bought your favourite books, don't forget to register with us to rate, review and join in the discussions

Visit **www.millsandboon.co.uk**
for all this and more today!